The Youngest Pilgrim

One Boy's Journey of Faith

J. G. "Jack" Green

New Hope
Birmingham, Alabama

New Hope
P. O. Box 12065
Birmingham, AL 35202-2065

 First printing 1991
Printed in the United States of America

Dewey Decimal Classification: JF
Subject Headings: CHRISTIAN LIFE—JUVENILE FICTION
CONVERSION—JUVENILE FICTION
Cover design by Dwayne Coleman

N914113•7.5M•0391

ISBN: 1-56309-001-5

Having enjoyed a pilgrimage blessed by God, this work is humbly dedicated to Mary Edna, my life partner of more than 45 years.

"His Burden loosed from off his shoulders, and fell from off his back, and began to tumble, and so continued to do, till it came to the mouth of the Sepulchre, where it fell in, and [he] saw it no more."

John Bunyan, *The Pilgrim's Progress*

Contents

Introduction

This fictional story is written with the specific intent of telling how a young Korean becomes a Christian. His conversion and experiences in living the Christian life reveal that life-shaping choices must be made by Christians. It reveals the influence older Christians may have on the young. My intent is to challenge the reader to consider his own life and the influence he may use to benefit others. I believe the ideology befitting Christians makes them enemies to certain other influences prevalent in the world today. These influences are revealed with a suggestion as to how they may be confronted.

The story is told in a Korean setting, using the cultural pattern of Korea. Last names will be first, as is the custom in Korea.

It is my prayer that God will be honored and souls enlightened as they read this story.

J. G. ("Jack") Green

CHAPTER 1

A Boy and His Friend

Lee, Yong-soo was a lad of only four when his mother began to send him down to the little corner store for simple orders. It was always something a little hand could hold and a young mind could remember.

It was there, where so many things looked attractive, that Yong first met the big, strong man who owned the store. He just knew his name to be Mr. Kim. That was sufficient for the simple transactions Yong needed to make.

After months of making such visits, Yong began to feel something very personal about Mr. Kim. He was always so kind and patient. It was more to see him than to get whatever his mother wanted which made Yong jump up from his play when asked to make a quick trip to the store.

There was something else about Mr. Kim which puzzled Yong. As he looked around at the goodies in the store, Yong noticed Mr. Kim had a big black book on the little table beside his chair.

At those times when he rushed in, he would find Mr. Kim reading the book. Yong wondered, What is he always reading? If I could read, I'd know what that book contained. One day I'll ask him.

That day did not come soon, however, and Yong thought about the book from time to time. Then one day while in the store for a quick visit, Yong was surprised to see that there were now *two* big books on the table! This puzzled Yong greatly. As he grew older, he noticed the two books were getting rather worn.

On every possible occasion he asked his mother for permission to go to the store; he promised not to touch anything or beg Mr. Kim for a gift, which was a temptation.

It was Yong's favorite place. Sometimes he would sit on the

little step to the store and Mr. Kim would join him. They talked about many things.

Frequently Mr. Kim would tell Yong about the "war" and the many years his beloved Korea had been divided. Yong noticed that his friend's voice dropped to a whisper when this subject was being discussed. It seemed painful for Mr. Kim. He would say something like, "I'm praying that we can end this 40 years of division and unify this beautiful country without war. We are trying to build a democracy, but it is so difficult when there is the constant threat from the North. Keeping so many soldiers prepared is expensive and sure slows our march toward democracy."

Yong did not understand all of this, but these talks were filed away in his memory as precious times; for this big friend was confiding his deepest thoughts with him.

Most of the time they talked about ordinary things like the weather. When it was hot, Yong would tell Mr. Kim he was fortunate to be down in the street where there was a breeze. As Yong grew older, Mr. Kim would give him a small broom and ask him to sweep the sidewalk. Yong knew Koreans were very proud of their cleanliness. He would ask Mr. Kim for the broom; that way he knew he could stay a little longer.

One day as Yong came into the store, he saw Mr. Kim with the big black book in his hand. Now that Yong was in school and learning to read and write, he thought he might be able to understand why Mr. Kim always had the book beside him. He wanted to know about the second book too, but for the time being he would be satisfied to know about the big black one.

Yong did not just come right out and ask about the book. He spent some time sweeping out the store and the sidewalk. He waited while Mr. Kim helped two customers. The store was a prominent gathering place for the Imja Dong community, and some of the women took quite a long time as they passed news of the families in the area to one another and to Mr. Kim.

Today Yong remembered how kind Mr. Kim had been to him all of these years. Surely Mr. Kim would not mind such a personal question as Yong was about to ask. He had to find out about that book, as it was so important to Mr. Kim, and Mr. Kim was so important to Yong-soo.

When Mr. Kim came to sit on the doorstep with Yong, the time seemed right. The conversation began as usual with questions about the family's health: what was Mother doing to get ready for the winter? and when was Daddy coming home? and how were Grandmother's stiff joints?

Then Yong decided to come right out with it. "Mr. Kim, I really like you. You are about the kindest friend a boy can have. I like to come down to your store and visit with you. But I have a big question I want to ask you, if it is all right."

Without hesitating a moment, the twinkle in his eye deepening to reflect the serious tone of the conversation, Mr. Kim replied, "Why certainly, Yong. You are my best friend too. What is the question you have burning in your mind and heart?"

"Well, sir," Yong said slowly now (for it was not good manners for a young man to pry into the affairs of a grown man of the business world), "I have noticed you always have a big black book on your table. I see you reading it when I come here for my purchases. We have been friends now for several years, and I've noticed you've about worn out the book. I thought if it's that important to you, I need to know about it. Sir, am I too personal, or can you tell me about that book?"

The twinkle returned to the shopkeeper's eye. He went to his table, picked up the book, and brought it to Yong. As he saw down beside his young friend, Yong noticed the words on the cover—*Holy Bible.* He had never seen either of the two words and his curiosity became apparent.

"Yong, we call this the God Book. It is a book that tells about God and how He wants us to live. There's so much in this book for me to learn, I read it daily. Yet each day I find something new. It is a remarkable book, and someday I hope you'll be able to read it."

The lad was stunned. He understood little of what Mr. Kim had said, except about the daily reading and something about how to live. That prompted him to blurt out, "Oh, Mr. Kim, you are about the best man I have ever met, and I don't think you need to read about how to live!"

Pleased at this response, Mr. Kim moved a little closer to Yong and put his arm around his shoulder. "My dear little friend, what I have learned from this book has changed my life. If there is anything I do that you like, it is because of God, and He tells me each day how to live when I read His book. Someday I will tell you what is in the book which may change your life too."

That was enough for one day. Yong had been visiting the store for years, but he felt this was the most important day of all. He had asked about the big black book. And though he did not understand much Mr. Kim said, Yong knew that it was an important book.

There was the question of the second book. Yong thought he would ask about that later. Now, as he bounded into his house, it was apparent to Mrs. Lee that her son had a new confidence in himself. As he played, she heard him mentioning how good it was to have smart friends. One day she would know her son had the most influential Friend a young man could have; One Who would help him live a life of love and spiritual success.

CHAPTER 2

A Family with Pride

Yong's small house was set against a little hill. There was a small area in the backyard where a boy could play, and a mother could hang her wash. The more spacious front yard was hard and swept clean.

There was a tree which gave some shade in the summer and stood tall and clean in the winter. Yong would climb the tree and look out over the city and the more than 2,000 persons who lived in Imja Dong.

He could see Mr. Kim's rooftop. That always gave him a good feeling when things got too hot or too crowded in the three rooms which made up the living and sleeping area of the house.

The kitchen was a small space in the back where Yong's mother, Oh, Soo-won, spent most of the day. Here she prepared the daily meals. Frequently the neighbors came over to prepare *kimchi* (hot cabbage) with her, sharing the latest news of other neighbors.

The most important person in the house was the matriarch of the family, Grandmother Kang, Gyong-ae. She came to the family home at the time of her husband's death. Like most Korean grandmothers, she became the one who gave formal and final instructions concerning the family's daily activities.

Kang, Gyong-ae was a kindly woman who took family matters seriously. Her eldest son, Lee, Soon-suk, had married Oh, Soo-won after proper consultations with those who were learned in the matters of matrimony. The matchmaker had been one of the oldest and most knowledgeable of all the elders of Imja Dong. He had said that the signs were right for a good and sound marriage to take place, one that would be blessed with a good boy child and much peace and happiness.

It was Grandmother who knew all the family secrets. Yong had been told from the earliest day how he would behave and how he would treat his elders. When questions about the dress and manners of others came up, it was always Grandmother who gave the formal interpretation as to the ultimate meaning of it all.

Yong heard all the folk songs, the favorites of the Korean people, as sung with the soft voice of Grandmother Kang. She never raised her voice when talking to Yong or her daughter-in-law Oh, Soo-won. Dignity seemed to mark the bearing of the small frame who knew in a moment how to handle family affairs.

There were matters Yong never discussed with Grandmother, even though they aroused his curiosity. He would not dare ask her about the beads she carried around and what she would be saying when there seemed to be no one listening. The whole matter seemed too personal. And besides, no mere lad should be listening at times like those, and certainly must not ask such questions of an elder.

Yong's father was absent most of the time. He worked for the railway system and was out of town about five days each week. When he came home, it was always a glad reunion. He would stop in the yard to find Yong, sweep him up in his arms, draw him to his strong chest, and ask, "How is my little man?" This made Yong proud.

Father would greet Grandmother when he entered the door, and the question would be, "How are your joints?" Father knew that Grandmother would tell him how difficult it was to get up and down. Both of them knew the days in the rice field had taken their toll. More and more, Grandmother was being drawn over; she had to be in pain, and a respectful son wanted to know about Mother.

There was warmth and appreciation in the eyes of Oh, Soo-won when she came out of the kitchen to greet her husband. They greeted with a smile, asking of each other's welfare. It was then Mother would bring matters needing attention to "Mr. Lee," as she called him. Grandmother would add her bit of final instruction at this time, making the homecoming complete.

Things that bothered the Lee family seldom came to Yong's attention. Father had such a good job working for the government-owned railway system that many of the financial problems his young friends heard about never came to his ears. Too, he was warned by Grandmother never to ask questions when things did not seem just right.

"All things will come to you, if you just wait," she said in her quiet, authoritarian voice. That satisfied Yong.

Therefore, when he stepped into the house after his visit with Mr. Kim and had learned about the book, it was as if he had found a fine and wonderful treasure. Like all boys who felt they had learned something special, it was hard for him to hide the fact.

Mother glanced at Grandmother when Yong came home that day. His was a proud family; and if one knew something important, it was necessary for all to share it, especially before neighbors heard about it.

"Yong, you have been to the corner store?" asked Grandmother, taking the burden of asking the question from his mother.

"Yes, Grandmother," was the simple and complete reply. Quickly, Yong picked up one of his toys, busying himself with it.

"Tell us, Yong, how is Mr. Kim?" asked Grandmother.

"Just fine," answered Yong, once again giving his attention to the toy.

"Well, put the toy away, son, and tell us what you and Mr. Kim have been talking about," she said in her quietly stern manner.

Yong did not know how to answer. He was not going to be rude to his wonderful grandmother, but some things were just too personal to share, even with such a family authority as she.

"Well, we talked about the weather, and I heard them telling of Mr. Choi's accident the other day when he fell in the ditch." He had not lied, but there was something he had not told them. He had not told about the book; he felt that was between Mr. Kim and himself.

At that moment the music from the radio stopped and the announcer said there was to be a special bulletin. The conversation was interrupted; there was complete quiet. The man on the radio said something about a soldier who came across the lines from North Korea as a defector. Details were being given, and Yong thought it was a timely interruption.

Quietly, hoping to avoid the interrogation further, Yong eased out of the house. The wind was turning colder now, and as he glanced up into the sky, he knew there was something he did not understand. He knew there was some difference between the beads that his grandmother held and seemed to talk to in her quiet moments and the book Mr. Kim said told him what to do when he read it.

The family of Lee, Yong-soo had much of which to be proud. This gave Yong reason to hold his head up when he went through the Dong. He had a father who worked hard and regularly, who came home to be with his mother at every occasion. He had a grandmother who seemed to know all about everything, and was kind to him as she shared her marvelous information. His faithful mother provided for her family with much dignity. She was esteemed in the community, and that was the reason the neighbors came to prepare their *kimchi* in her kitchen.

Now Yong had a secret. It made him proud to know a man like Mr. Kim would share with him the secrets of his personal life. For Yong it meant it was good to be alive and to have a family like his and a friend like Mr. Kim.

CHAPTER 3

A Life-changing Crisis

Life seemed marvelous for Yong; the years skipped by without difficulty. It was in the early summer of his twelfth year that it changed suddenly.

School dismissed for the summer holidays. As Yong cleaned out his desk for the last time, he was glad he had gotten the best marks on his studies for the year. The family would be proud of him. He was anxious to get home to tell the good news.

Usually Yong-soo would meet his best friend, Cho, Soon-sik, and they would kick a ball around the school yard before heading home. Today, however, was a day when Yong knew he wanted to get home early. Now that school was in recess, there would be other days when they could play.

"Where are you going in such a hurry, Yong?" Soon-sik yelled as they were dashing out the front door of the school. "We should have many of our classmates staying today to play with us. We can go against the older boys today, and maybe we can beat them this time."

Yong did not hesitate, but shouted over his shoulder he had to get home early. He wanted to tell his mother and grandmother about his school marks, and then he needed to talk to Mr. Kim before he closed the store for the evening.

With this quick exchange, the two boys separated. Yong headed home.

Climbing the hillside, he got a glimpse of a large manly figure in his yard. It was not the weekend and Father would not be there—or would he? But, yes, it was his father! Now what would cause him to come home early?

Running quickly, Yong came breathlessly to a halt when he saw the look on his father's face. His strong face, with weather lines etched in just the right places, was drawn and pale. Yong thought, What could have brought such a change to the most handsome face in all of Imja Dong?

Father saw Yong-soo come into the yard and half turned from greeting him. This was unusual. Yong decided his father was not going to speak. He would run to Grandmother, for she always had time and spoke so plainly of matters difficult to understand.

It was at this moment Yong-soo received the shock of his life. His dear grandmother was not in her corner on her favorite pallet. Where was she? Why was Father home so soon?

Then came the tender voice of Yong's mother. "Yong, come here to the back room. I heard you come in and I know you're looking for your grandmother. She's not here. They came for her. She's not coming back." Yong could hear the sob in Mother's throat. He was frightened. He was stunned at seeing Father home early and Grandmother not in her corner and, now, the voice of his dear mother breaking into a sob.

Who came for Grandmother? Where did they take her? Why isn't she coming back? This was Yong's first encounter with death. He had never heard much about Grandfather Lee and certainly nothing about his death.

There was quiet in the Lee household. The candles were lit and people came and went, always speaking in hushed tones. They brought food and some brought little white envelopes to give to Yong's father.

It seemed so unfair. He left Grandmother well and happy when we went to school; he had come home and she was gone. What could a boy of 12 expect to learn from all of this, and who would take the time to tell him?

The warm sunshine sparkled against the dust that was raised when the cars came toward the house. Every time Yong saw the dust clouds, he thought about Mr. Kim's store and the need to use the little broom.

Mr. Kim! thought Yong. He's the one who will tell me about Grandmother. He can tell me what it means. Why didn't I think of him earlier?

The older folk were busy, though Yong did not know any of the things they were doing or talking about; none of them knew he was around. It would be a good time to visit Mr. Kim. He slipped off down the hill to his friend's store.

Neither would be aware of it, but a lifelong bond was about to be established between Lee, Yong-soo and Kim, Kye-taek which would be meaningful beyond explanation for both of them. In fact, it would be life-changing for Yong.

When Mr. Kim looked up from measuring rice, he noticed his young friend leaning against the door. Yong's back was to the inside; he was slumped in appearance. Mr. Kim had heard about Yong's grandmother, for nothing escaped the discussions at the corner store. It was not raw gossip, but a benevolent keeping up with the goings and comings of people who care for one another.

"Yong, I want you to know how sorry I was to hear about your grandmother," Mr. Kim said. He could not see the lad's face. If he had been able to see it, he would have noticed a tear ease down the smooth and youthful cheek. Wiping the tear quickly, Yong tried to reply, but couldn't.

Now Mr. Kim's age and experience began emerging. Yong-soo remembered it for years to come. Without another word, Mr. Kim stepped to the store entrance and put his arm around Yong. He led him gently back to a chair by the old table, placing him in it with a tenderness that spoke to Yong's heart.

"Yong, do you remember asking me about my old black book?" Mr. Kim said quietly. Yong's first thought was, Why such a question at a time like this? What would that book have to do with Grandmother's death? Yet, knowing the wisdom and kindness of Mr. Kim, Yong controlled his thoughts long enough to answer, "Yes, sir."

"Well, I told you my life was controlled by God Who spoke to me through that book. I told you someday I would tell you what was in the book. The time has come, but first let me tell you some things you do not know about me."

Mr. Kim told Yong why he closed his little store each Sunday. He told of his weekly visits on Sundays and Wednesdays to a red-brick building in the center of Imja Dong. Yong had seen the building and even heard singing come from there when he went down to the big market with his mother on Sundays. He had heard some of his friends talking about the building and calling it a church.

"Yong," Mr. Kim continued, "I must tell you about my family. You have never met my wife. You will never meet her, for she is dead. My two daughters are dead too." This news was too much for Yong. His sorrow almost overwhelmed him, and great sobs filled his chest.

"Do you want me to continue?" Mr Kim asked quietly.

"Yes, please do," replied Yong, now almost pleading for a time of sharing.

"My wife and daughters were at home not too far from here on the other side of the small hill. I was away at the time attending to some business matters. A great typhoon came through Imja Dong. The water brought the wall down behind the house, and the earth from the hill completely covered our home. It came so suddenly that my family did not survive.

"Yong, I wanted to die. Some time later a friend told me about the red-brick building standing in the center of Imja Dong, which is called a church. Out of my heartache and need, I went to church one Sunday morning. I heard about a man called Jesus Christ. I did not understand any of it, but I noticed a book that many took home with them when they left the church. I inquired of them, and they told me it was a Bible and told me where I could purchase one for myself."

It was now a time of simple sharing; there was openness and oneness between a man and his young friend. They sat in the semi-darkness of the little store whispering while touching souls. Questions which would have taken years to be asked came easily now from Yong's heart.

Yong's secret had become even greater now. He asked one question which seemed to fill Mr. Kim with gladness. "Mr. Kim, you tell me you finally found peace about death. It would seem that I am old enough for you to tell me about how you got that peace. Do you think you could tell me?"

"First," Mr. Kim replied, "I want you to ask your mother if you can go with me next Sunday. You don't have to be concerned about your clothes or any money. If you can go, I'll stop by and speak to your folks on Sunday and take you to church. It will be about 10:30. We'll be back about 1:00."

This was the greatest invitation Yong had ever received. He would be able to be with the finest friend a young man could have; going to a very special place where a young fellow who had just lost his wonderful grandmother could find peace and maybe learn to understand it.

In spite of the pall of gloom which hung heavy over the Lee home, there seemed to be a ray of light around Yong-soo. He seemed as happy as when he was at his grandmother's knee. The family would not have understood it, even if they had had time to notice it.

Yong did not know how all of this was to shape his life in the days to come. Mr. Kim may have known; but if he did, he told no one. Yong had no idea of the great adventure that lay ahead!

CHAPTER 4

The Great Adventure

Seldom had Yong heard his mother preparing breakfast. He was always sleeping. The first thing he heard was the pleasant call she gave when breakfast was ready.

On this particular day, however, Yong heard the rooster crow in the distance and someone in the Dong yelling and running. He had never heard those people before, even though he heard stories about the exercises that had become so popular early in the mornings.

Today was different! Yong heard everything. It seemed his mother would never call him to breakfast. When the time came, Mother knew Yong was acting just a little peculiar. He was awake before she called. He jumped right out of his pallet bed, ready for breakfast in record time.

Having been busy with Grandmother's funeral, Mother had not noticed Yong for several days. Now he was up and around before breakfast. It wasn't like him; he had taken the loss of his grandmother very hard. She would have to inquire about his welfare.

It did not take her long to find out what her son had on his mind. When he came to breakfast, he was dressed in his best clothes.

"Mother," Yong almost whispered,"you remember Mr. Kim is coming by this morning to take me to church, don't you? He did speak to you the other day about my going with him today, didn't he?"

"So that's it," Mother replied. "I've been thinking maybe you were not feeling well. This is the first time I can remember you were awake before I called. This must be something really special you and Mr. Kim are going to do today. Yes, I remember he asked if he could have my permission to take you to his church. He said he would take care of you and bring you straight home after church."

This is how the day began, but neither mother nor son knew just how special this day was going to be for the Lee family.

It seemed as though Mr. Kim would never come. When the hour finally arrived, Mr. Lee was the first to greet the shopkeeper. "Well, Mr. Kim, I think it is a fine thing for you to take time with our son. He has really looked forward to this day. His mother says she had to call him only once today to get him out of bed. We didn't have to drag him over to the bathhouse either. Yes, it must be *something great* you are going to do today."

Mr. Kim smiled broadly and said, "Well, we do have a good time at our church, and I've told Yong something about it. I guess I may have gotten just a little too excited about today. But I will watch after him and bring him home about 1:30, if that's all right with you."

Mr. Lee took this time to tell Mr. Kim how much the Lee family appreciated him and how he had been such a good shopkeeper. The two men seemed to have a deep and kindly regard for each other and stood sharing their respect for some time in mutual courtesies.

Then, it was off to church for Yong and Mr. Kim. Somehow, as he looked up to the tall, old friend, Yong felt taller and more important than he had ever felt in his life. To have a grown man take him to his own church, and to know there was a bond between them few people could understand . . . with this thought Yong's heart swelled almost to the bursting point. This was a great day; what an adventure!

When they arrived at the big red-brick building, people were coming from all directions to enter it. There were old people, middle-aged people, young people, and some other children. Everybody seemed happy and looked clean and dressed up. Now, Yong thought, this is why Mother insisted I get all clean and dressed properly. She knew how these people would look.

Mr. Kim seemed to know everyone. He bowed and spoke to all the family members he met, and smiled that big broad smile he always had when greeting his customers.

As they entered the building, a man handed Mr. Kim a piece of paper. He asked for another one, and gave it to Yong. It had a lot of typed words on it.

Mr. Kim, speaking softly, said, "Yong, this is our program for today. Keep it, and you can follow what is happening during the worship service." Yong did not know all he heard, but he knew this had to be an important paper, and he would keep it to show to his mother when he got home.

Someone opened the door for Mr. Kim and Yong; they went into the room where everyone was seated on benches. Some were talking, while others were reading the program. As soon as they were seated, someone began to play the large organ at the front of the room. Yong had seen an organ at his school auditorium, but this one was larger than any he had seen, and it sounded so good!

It reminded Yong he had seen his school principal entering the church at the same time he and Mr. Kim had arrived. He was the only person that Yong recognized in the large crowd, even though there were faces he had seen in the market from time to time.

Looking around, Yong noticed that most people had two books. One was like Mr. Kim's, but he did not recognize the other book. He soon learned this was the book used when singing.

When the organ music stopped, a man stepped to the front and called out a number. The people turned to that number in the book, and for the first time he noticed Mr. Kim had two books. He opened the smaller book to the page and held it down where Yong could follow it. Yong wondered about this, because other than the songs Grandmother taught him, he had never done much singing.

Now it seemed every person in the group was singing. Yong had never heard this many people singing together before. It was beautiful! He listened to Mr. Kim's singing and did his best to follow him. It surprised him how easy it was to follow the tune with Mr. Kim, the crowd, the organ, and the piano all singing and playing at the same time. Yong felt he would never forget this grand experience.

The strangest thing for Yong occurred after the singing. A man came to the desk up on the big platform and asked the group to bow their heads. Mr. Kim whispered to Yong, "We are going to pray now, just bow your head and close your eyes."

With every head bowed and all the eyes closed (Yong had to peek out to see if everyone was doing what they had been asked to do), the man began to talk out loud. He opened with, "God, our Father." This really puzzled Yong, and he wondered who the man was addressing. He had never heard anything like this in his life.

The man talked by himself for nearly five minutes. Yong wondered if everyone knew what the man was doing. As soon as he finished, Mr. Kim whispered to Yong, "This man is the pastor of the church. We will hear more from him later."

There was more singing. Then some men passed velvet bags to each person and they put money into them. Mr. Kim put in an envelope full of money. The odd thing was Yong had not heard anyone ask for money. He assumed this was something everyone knew they would do and had come prepared for it.

When the large group of people behind the pastor began singing, their unity amazed Yong. They were together as if they were one voice. There was a singing group at his school, but they did not compare to these people. He had never heard a group sing like this, and with all the other things he was experiencing, he sat in church in wonder.

Mr. Kim told Yong in his quiet voice, "They are one of our choirs and they sing every week." Yong would always remember the song they sang, for it was to be the first one he learned for himself. "Amazing Grace" became his favorite song. When he heard the choir, he knew nothing of the meaning of the words, but he knew it was beautiful.

The one Mr. Kim had called pastor stood up to speak, and Yong saw he had one of those big black books exactly like Mr. Kim's! He opened it and began to read.

He read about a little man who wanted to see a famous person coming down the street and he could not see over the crowd. He had to climb a tree. The pastor called the famous person Jesus Christ.

This was the same man Mr. Kim had mentioned to Yong, the man of *the book.* Yong listened as hard as he could. It was a fine story and had a beautiful ending. The pastor said Jesus Christ went home with the little man who climbed the tree. Then he said, "Jesus will go home with you if you will let Him."

Yong heard very little else that morning. He was deep in thought about what the pastor had said about Jesus and the little man. He would have to ask Mr. Kim about this on the way home.

It was some time before everything was finished. There was more singing and more words spoken with heads bowed. Then Mr. Kim led Yong out the front of the church. He went from group to group shaking hands and saying words of greeting.

The pastor stood at the entrance to the worship area. He was speaking to those who wanted to shake his hand. When Yong and Mr. Kim got to the door, Mr. Kim introduced Yong to the pastor.

"Pastor, this is my friend Lee, Yong-soo. You know his father, Lee, Soon-suk, who is supervisor for the railway system. He comes from a fine family. Yong's grandmother died recently and I asked Yong to come to church with me today. We are going to help him understand something about being a Christian. This is his first visit with us."

Yong's life seemed to have flashed before his mind as Mr. Kim spoke. Yet he was so proud to have such a friend who could make such a grand introduction. Yong was to remember the introduction in the days to come.

"Yong-soo," the pastor replied, "we are so glad you came with our Mr. Kim today. He's a wonderful Christian, and you're honored to have such a friend. You may come back any time you desire. We'll always be happy to have you with us. Too, I want you to know all about our church and our Lord, Jesus Christ."

There was another word Yong did not understand—*Lord.* He had read about men being called lords, but that was ancient history, and he had some stories in his schoolbooks about them. Now he heard the word again, and in church. What could it mean?

This was just one of several questions burning Yong's heart. He had much to ask Mr. Kim; he could hardly wait to get started home. He had to have the answers before he talked to his mother because she would ask him, and he did not want to appear uninformed.

As they moved out of the church, Yong watched as Mr. Kim spoke to those standing in small groups in front of the church. There were questions about the health and welfare of family members. There was polite bowing and courteous compliments being passed to those who greeted each other. This was impressive to the young mind of the visitor. Everyone seemed so friendly! Yong would remember that it was good to see so many people smiling, shaking hands, and saying kind things to each other.

As soon as their feet turned toward home, Yong began to ask his older friend questions. There was much he wanted to know about church. Who were all of those people? What were they singing about? Why did they give money? What was the man doing who talked out loud with his head bowed and eyes closed? Who was the little man who climbed the tree and why did he want to see Jesus? Why did the pastor call Jesus Lord?

The questions rolled off Yong's tongue so rapidly, Mr. Kim had to chuckle. "Hold up a minute, son," Mr. Kim said, giving Yong a signal to stop the questions. He had a familiar smile on his face, for he was happy to see his young friend so interested in the events at the church.

"I am not quite ready to answer all of those questions just yet. Yong, you have four more days before school begins. If you will come down to the store tomorrow, we'll begin answering some of those questions. Today, I just want you to think about this great adventure. I want you to think about all you've heard and see if anything comes to your mind which will clear up what you have asked."

The two fell silent, but Yong's head was spinning. He busied himself trying to match strides with Mr. Kim on the way home, even though the older friend's legs were much longer. It seemed to take Yong's mind off his questions. The racing of his mind seemed to slow somewhat, and as only two friends can do, they walked without speaking a word, side by side, up the hill to Yong's house.

It was a great sight to see the older man holding the hand of his young friend. Something wonderful had happened that day to make the bond between the two unbreakable for the years ahead.

When Yong's mother greeted them and thanked Mr. Kim, she saw the joy on her son's face. She knew immediately the great adventure of the day would be something her only child would treasure. She did not know the details, and Yong did not seem to want, or be able, to share. Yet, as only mothers could discern, she saw something in the heart of her son she had not detected before.

One day she would find out all about the Sunday he had spent with Mr. Kim. It was, however, not the last of the great days for the two friends.

Yong made one statement about the day. "Mother, I had a wonderful time and I want to go again next Sunday, if you give your permission."

In the light of all the sad times the Lee family had know recently, it was good to see joy and happiness.

Mother decided she could learn of her son's experience later, when he was ready to share. Little did she know this was the beginning of a new life for her only son, the opening of a new era for the Lee family.

For Yong it had been a great adventure. He looked forward to the time when he would sit down with Mr. Kim and learn the meaning of all he had seen, heard, and felt.

CHAPTER 5

A Day of Learning

The Monday following his first visit to the church, Yong had one thought, When can I see Mr. Kim? His mother had asked several questions about church, but there was little Yong could tell her. He had to get some answers from Mr. Kim if any sense could be made of his experience.

"Mother, I promised Mr. Kim I'd come sweep the store for him today, and we'd talk about yesterday. He told me he'd explain some of the things I saw and heard. Don't be alarmed if I'm there most of the day. We have much to talk about."

Not waiting for a reply, Yong hurtled through the door, off to see his friend. He heard Mother give him permission as he ran across the yard. Like all good mothers, she gave Yong a word of warning not to bother the good shopkeeper or get in his way.

On Mondays Mr. Kim received new items for the store. The truck had arrived, and the task of putting up new stock had begun when Yong got to the store.

"Good morning, Mr. Kim. How are you today? It's a pretty day today, isn't it?" These seemed rhetorical questions, since Yong was not waiting for a reply.

Mr. Kim appreciated the enthusiasm. It seemed to give a great lift to his spirit. "Well, good morning, Yong. How are you today? I didn't expect you quite so early, but I am glad to see you."

Yong noticed Mr. Kim would be too busy to talk unless he had some help with his new stock. Without being asked, Yong opened one of the boxes and found the place for the new merchandise. As he was doing this, he noticed that Mr. Kim seemed pleased to have a helper.

Customers filtered in and out of the store, interrupting Mr. Kim from stock duties. Yong continued to stock the shelves. When he finished, he took the broom and swept the floor, putting water on the sidewalk to keep the dust from the store. Lastly, he wiped the dust from the fruit and stacked it neatly.

He did this with one purpose in mind. The sooner the work was completed, the sooner the questions which burned Yong's heart could be answered.

Anticipating Yong's anxiety, Mr. Kim took the initiative to open the discussion. "Well, Yong, how did you sleep last night?"

While this seemed a strange way to open an important conversation, Yong replied, "I slept very well."

"Did you have any thoughts about your experience in church?" Mr. Kim asked, showing no expression in his voice.

"Yes, sir, I did remember you said I needed to think about some things in my quiet time. I thought about how beautifully the people sang and the happiness I saw in the faces of those people at church. But I still don't know the answers to those questions I asked on the way home."

Mr. Kim picked up his Bible from the little table. "OK, Yong, come over here and sit beside me. We have much to talk about in these next few days, and many of those questions will be answered."

Yong was beside Mr. Kim in a flash. The questions he asked yesterday were just a few of the things he'd been thinking about since the death of his grandmother. He knew Mr. Kim was the smartest, kindest man he had ever known. Now there would be a time of personal instruction and teaching.

"We need to talk about the little man in the tree, Yong. It was the story Pastor Choi read from the Bible yesterday. Well, it is written in one of the divisions of the Bible, which we call books. There are 66 books in the Bible. There are 39 in the first part of the Bible, which is the Old Testament; and 27 in the second part of the Bible, called the New Testament."

Mr. Kim continued, "It is the New Testament which tells about the life of Jesus Christ. It has the story about the little man in it. We'll learn more about the Bible, but first let's talk about the story Pastor read yesterday. You remember the name of the man, don't you? It was Zacchaeus."

The Bible was now open in Mr. Kim's gentle hands. "This man, while not big in stature, was a very prominent citizen, Yong. It is recorded here that he was a rich man. He was surprised when Jesus looked up and told him to come down out of the tree, telling him He wanted to go home with him."

Yong interrupted, "Why did Jesus want to go home with him, Mr. Kim? He hardly knew him, did he?" It was here that Kim, Kye-taek showed his wisdom and understanding of a young mind. He did not rush in with an answer, but thoughtfully put his hand under his chin and just let the question rest between the two of them.

Finally, the silence, which seemed long for Yong, was broken as the dear Christian gentleman began the story that Yong was to keep in his heart for the rest of his life on earth.

"Yong, the one thing I had to learn about Jesus was that He was sent to our world by His Father. He was God and man in human form. We are told in the Bible God made the heavens and the earth. In fact, we learn God knows everything about everything, since He made it. Jesus was the Son of God. He knew everything about every person He ever met. Zacchaeus did not know much about Jesus, but Jesus knew everything about him."

Since it was Mr. Kim who was making these statements, Yong never thought about doubting them. He was concerned about understanding what his friend was saying. "You mean Jesus knows who our families are and what we are thinking?"

"Yes, and more, Yong," was the simple reply.

Then came the moment Mr. Kim knew was to be very important in future conversations. It was to be memorable for Yong. Mr. Kim explained, "Jesus went home with the rich man. Many people did not understand why Jesus would visit such a home. They thought since Zacchaeus was a tax collector and had gotten his money by cheating many of the people, that Jesus should not have anything to do with him.

"You will learn, Yong, many things Jesus did were not understood by the people. There were some leaders called Jews, who were of Jesus' own race and religion, who got very angry and frightened about such activities. As we study, you will also learn Jesus did what His Father wanted Him to do—treat everyone with love. This meant He would go home with many He met. Some would enjoy a meal with Him. Others would be healed of their illnesses. All would know the truth about God, life, and death."

"Zacchaeus knew he was in the presence of a very important religious leader. Remember he said very quickly that he would return all the money he had taken four times over and give half of all he owned to the poor people. It was as though he knew Jesus was able to know all about his past. He felt guilty and sorry for what he'd done. He wanted it corrected. This is repentance. Yet even with his repayment, he couldn't change the past; he needed forgiveness. It is very important, Yong, to know how to repent. When done properly, it is always followed by forgiveness. You'll learn that Jesus died on the cross to make that forgiveness possible."

Before Yong could ask any further questions, Mr. Kim closed his Bible and turned to look into Yong's face. "Son, I want you to know how concerned I am for your peace of mind and heart. We had a fine time yesterday, and for you to have those questions answered I must tell you about Jesus. When you know Jesus Christ personally, you will understand the singing, praying, and giving of money. In fact, you will learn all about church and worship."

The words had a finality about them. Mr. Kim looked tired, and Yong knew he had been there quite a long time. Without saying a word, Yong rose to leave. He remembered the soft drink and box of cookies Mr. Kim had provided for a snack lunch and gave a polite thanks. He glanced out to see the dirt on the sidewalk again and thought how he would have a good reason to come tomorrow.

Yong would have no need for a reason, however, for Mr. Kim said, "I will look for you tomorrow, Yong. Today has been a day of learning. We'll learn more about Jesus, and I'm sure one day you'll be able to meet Him personally. Come early tomorrow. I have a very special gift for you."

The last statement fell like a bomb on Yong's ears. A gift? What could it be?

Lee, Yong-soo rushed out of the store with a loud and joyful, "Thank you, Mr. Kim, I'll be here early tomorrow!"

CHAPTER 6

A Gift for Life

When Yong-soo rushed into his house, Mother was preparing supper. "Mother, I've had a wonderful day. What do you need for me to do to help you get supper ready?" Yong was so excited, he was yelling. The news of the gift from Mr. Kim thrilled him.

Mother knew something wonderful had happened, but she did not want to seem too interested. Young sons needed some secrets, and wise mothers respected such secrecy. Yong's mother was wise.

With restraint she said, "Get the chopsticks and the bowls for the rice and put them on the table. We'll have supper in a few minutes and you can tell me all about your wonderful day."

The two sat with folded legs, eating the fine meal Mother had prepared. Yong's mind was active. He did not know it, but he spoke so his Mother could hear, even though he was speaking to himself.

"I wonder what gift Mr. Kim has for me?" Mother thought it time for a question of her own.

"Yong, did you say Mr. Kim has a gift for you? When did he tell you he would give it to you?"

Yong was startled at the question. He was not aware he had spoken so Mother could hear. He had been thinking so strongly about the gift. "What? Did I say something about a gift from Mr. Kim?"

"Yes, you did, and I feel you should tell me about the gift."

"Mother, Mr. Kim told me he had a gift for me. He said he would give it to me tomorrow." Yong spoke rather slowly as if he were giving out some very precious information. In fact, as he spoke, he wondered what that gift might be.

The tone of Yong's voice, with his manner of speaking, prompted his mother to change the conversation. She mentioned school opening for the new term, how the weather would be turning colder, what they would need to do to prepare for the changing season.

Soon it was off to bed. The long days were about over for this summer, but there was just enough lingering daylight for Yong to be able to glance at the graying skies of early evening streaked with a fading redness from the sun. Thoughts about that gift came to him again. He consoled himself by thinking he'd find out tomorrow, if it ever came. It seemed like such a long time since he had left the store in the afternoon.

When the call to breakfast came, Yong was out of bed with an early morning energy most boys do not have in late summer. After he slipped into his trousers and T-shirt and splashed some water on his face from a pan in the little washroom by the kitchen, he ran his wet hands through his beautiful black hair, making it look acceptable. He was ready for breakfast and a visit to the corner store.

After the usual greeting to his mother, the two settled down to a breakfast of warm rice and fresh fish soup. Gulping down his barley tea, Yong started to rise, only to feel a restraining hand from his mother.

"Just a minute, son," she almost whispered. "Don't you think you need to stay around here and help me just a bit before going down to the store? Give Mr. Kim some time to get the store in order and take care of his early morning customers. Too, you have neglected your young friends since the death of your grandmother. As you are about to begin school again, it would be nice of you to spend some time with your schoolmates."

"But, Mother," Yong whined with pain in his voice, "today is the day Mr. Kim is going to give me the gift. I know he's expecting me early this morning. Besides, I help him get the store ready for the day, and I'm not in his way. I'll take some time this afternoon to see my friends. They have been on holiday too and they haven't been here calling for me, have they?"

It was a slight nod of permission that Yong's mother gave, but he saw it. Many times he had seen his mother give that kind of nod as he was growing up in a home of love. Without waiting for more approval, he jumped up and started for the door.

"Yong, don't stay as long as you did yesterday. You don't want the neighbors talking about you and Mr. Kim being together too long each day. Remember, there are many who come into the store, and we don't want them to think you're taking up too much time from the good man."

Mr. Kim had been expecting Yong for some time and had, in

fact, gone to the door of the shop several times to see if his young friend was coming down the street.

"Good morning, Mr. Kim," yelled Yong, before getting to the store. He had seen the shopkeeper looking down the street and wanted him to know he was coming.

"Good morning, Yong. It is such a lovely day, and I've been expecting you for some time. Did you have some chores to do before you came?"

"No, sir, but I did talk with Mother about my daily trips to the store. She is afraid I'm taking too much of your time. She doesn't want the neighbors talking about my being down here too much."

He was now able to tell Mr. Kim anything about his family matters. That was a sense of relief as Grandmother had warned him not to tell too much about those things to those not in the family.

"Well," Mr. Kim replied, "that is very thoughtful of your mother, but I must tell her you are a great help around here. You sweep out the store, clean our sidewalk, making this the cleanest shop in all of Imja Dong. Many of my customers have remarked how much help you are to them when I'm busy. I believe they appreciate having you here to help me. Maybe I should talk to your mother about this matter."

That discussion took Yong's mind from the main item of the day—the gift Mr. Kim was going to give him. When *would* he give it to him? It would be rude for Yong to mention it, yet it was all he could do to keep from reminding Mr. Kim of his promise.

Mr. Kim's wisdom in personal affairs was beyond understanding. Without another word, he reached under the counter for a package. It was wrapped in shining silver paper with a large blue bow ribbon on the top.

When Yong saw it, he thought it had to be the most beautiful gift he'd ever seen!

Handing Yong the package, Mr. Kim looked into his little friend's eyes. He spoke with strong conviction. "Yong, I understand you have a birthday coming in two weeks. Well, this is just a little early, but I want to be the first to give you a gift. I asked your father when he was home last weekend when you'd be 13 years old, and he told me. This is such a special time, I just had to give you a special gift."

When Mr. Kim finished, Yong let out a long and meaningful, "Thank you, Mr. Kim!"

Until a few days ago, he thought his father was the smartest and kindest man in the world. Now Mr. Kim had given Yong reason to believe there were other men who were smart and kind. He knew it was great to have two such men helping him in life.

"May I open it now, sir?" Not waiting for an answer, Yong began slowly untying the bow on the beautiful package. He was careful with the ribbon and paper because "Mother will certainly want to keep this for future use."

Small hands sometimes have difficulty with precious things. This was no exception. Taking care not to tear the paper or ruin the ribbon, Yong finally removed the wrapping. At first glance he recognized the gift. He had seen one exactly like it on Mr. Kim's table for many years.

"Oh, Mr. Kim," Yong was almost in tears, "you have given me a Holy Bible exactly like yours. This must be a very expensive gift. I do not deserve such a wonderful gift. Please accept my humble thanks, for you have touched my heart. I shall prize this gift all my life and will remember you each time I read it."

The speech came straight from Yong's heart. Mr. Kim was deeply touched at Yong's expression of appreciation. Very slowly, he began to tell Yong the real meaning and purpose of the gift.

"Lee, Yong-soo, I want you to get to know Jesus one day. I want you to know His Book. We must study it together, and each Sunday we'll go to hear Pastor Choi tell us what God is saying to us from this book. I felt you had to have your very own Bible. Someday we'll get you a personal hymnal. Right now, I want you to open the book to the first few pages and let me help you with something you must do in the next few days."

Yong's fingers were pulling the covers of the book apart, trying to find the proper place as Mr. Kim had indicated. He found what he thought to be the right page. There were strange words on the page. "Mr. Kim, if this is the right page, I'll need some help because I've never seen these words before."

After waiting on a customer, Mr. Kim eased into his chair by his table and opened his own Bible. He began to pronounce the words, which he explained to be the names of the books. He reminded his young friend of his explanation about the books of the Bible.

"Now, Yong, I want you to memorize these book names. This is the order in which they appear in the Bible. You can't study the Bible unless you know where to find the things we'll discuss."

These two friends sat and discussed this most precious gift for a long time. Mr. Kim told about the meaning of words like *Genesis* and *Matthew*. It was fascinating for Yong, and once again the time had slipped away. As he started to excuse himself, thanking his wise and thoughtful friend for about the tenth time for his gift, he remembered the story of the little man in the tree.

"Mr. Kim, can you tell me where I can find the story about Zacchaeus and help me find it?" asked Yong. Delighted his young friend remembered their previous conversation, Mr. Kim opened the new Bible to the book of Luke. He explained that Luke was a medical doctor. The book bearing his name had many great stories about Jesus in it. Now he needed to explain about chapters, and how each thought was divided into sentences called verses.

"Yong, we are looking at the Gospel of Luke, chapter 19, verses 1 through 10. It will seem like a short story when you read it for yourself. Take your time; read it over and over again, and we'll talk about it tomorrow."

Tomorrow. That was the magic word for Yong. He remembered the admonition of his mother about staying too long. Too, he wanted her to see his gift.

He moved quickly to the door, pausing long enough to bow very deeply to Mr. Kim, expressing with that bow his deep and abiding appreciation for such a wonderful gift.

Lee, Yong-soo knew the gift he had received was one which would bind them together for life. Grandmother had said, "Some events make people friends for life." This fit her description of such an act. He felt wonderfully blessed to have such a thoughtful friend who knew all about God and was kind enough to give him a Holy Bible.

"Not many fellows have a friend like Mr. Kim. I'm fortunate!" With this great feeling in his heart, Yong turned his feet toward the hill leading to his home.

CHAPTER 7

New and Inspiring Things

When Yong arrived at his yard, he began calling with an excited voice for his mother to come see his wonderful gift. If she had not known about Mr. Kim's intention to give Yong the gift, she would have thought he had met some terrible accident.

She rushed to the door. The happiness was fresh and joyous; it had not been seen in the Lee household since Grandmother's death.

"Look, Mother, Mr. Kim gave me my very own Bible. Isn't it about the best gift anybody ever received? We've been reading it. There's much in the Bible I want to learn. I've got the best friend in the world in Mr. Kim. He said Father told him my birthday was just two weeks away, and this was an early gift!"

Yong's mother took the book in her hands to examine it carefully. Then in her quiet and thoughtful manner said, "Yong, this is a precious gift. Mr. Kim paid much money for this present. But this is more than an expensive gift; it seems like a *priceless* gift. You have been given the book that explains why Mr. Kim is such an honest and thoughtful man. I don't know what it says, but perhaps one day after you learn from it, you can tell Mother."

The expression of kindness and love almost overwhelmed Yong. He had never heard his mother speak in such terms. Tears came to his eyes. It was a wonderful day!

As a young man will do, he broke the spell. "Mother, Mr. Kim taught me how to pronounce the big words which he called books of the Bible.

"We discussed their names, and he told me he would teach me what the Bible says about God and His Son, Jesus Christ. Someday I can tell you what I learn, if you want to know."

It was then Yong's mother remembered an event of the day. She had a message for her son. "By the way, one of your classmates came by to see you today. He said he saw you in church last Sunday and wanted to talk to you about a Bible class they had for your age group. He said if he did not see you here at home, he would see you in school or at church. He gave me his name; it was Chang, Hee-sung."

"*Chang, Hee-sung?* Mother, he's the most popular boy in our school. You mean *he* came by to see *me?* When did he say he would come back? I didn't see him last Sunday; but there were so many people there, and everything was so new."

These were almost nonstop and rambling statements. A precious gift from a dear friend and the most popular boy in his school coming to see him with an invitation to become part of a Bible class—what more could happen in a single day?

When Yong slipped into his bed that night, his mind was in a whirl. He was so tired he went to sleep almost immediately, with just a short time to wonder what the future would hold.

In the days to come Yong had little time for anything except school. On Sundays he joined Mr. Kim at the foot of his little hill and the two walked to church together.

In the second week he found Chang, Hee-sung's Bible class offer to be a wonderful opportunity to get started learning the Bible.

Before school began, Yong spent the better part of those four days at the store with Mr. Kim. All these Bible studies left Yong with the impression there was much to learn; and he had a long way to go before he could match Mr. Kim, or even Chang, Hee-sung, in knowledge about the Bible.

On Sundays Pastor Choi read a portion of the Bible and told what it meant. More and more, Yong began to hear the Bible stories with a new ear. He was introduced to the book of John in the Friday evening Bible class. The teacher would ask each of his ten students to read from the Bible. He would then explain the meaning of each statement.

When something too difficult to understand came up in Bible class or in church, Yong would mark it in his Bible and take it to Mr. Kim, for he was to Yong the *final authority* on the Word of God.

There was always something lingering in Yong's mind about these misunderstood portions of the Scriptures. He knew something was not complete, or his understanding was lacking. Yet he could not put his finger on the exact cause for the feeling he had in his heart.

The days passed more quickly than any previous year for Yong. He met his friend Cho, Soon-sik and they kicked the ball around and did some idle talk about school. Soon-sik knew something was taking up much of Yong's time; but since he had never been to church, he did not know how to question him about it.

After a short time each day, Yong made an excuse about having to get home early. This was unusual because Yong was the one who usually insisted that Soon-sik remain on the playground until late in the afternoon.

Yong's mind floated between the questions he had for his Bible teacher and the things he would discuss with Mr. Kim. He was working hard on his school studies. He was one of the best students in his class, but there was much to think about these days.

When time came for his annual class party, Yong thought it would give him an opportunity to talk to his best friend about all he had been experiencing. This would explain why he had been leaving the playground early each day. Too, he could tell Soon how Mr. Kim had been helping him. Soon-sik knew Mr. Kim had given Yong much personal help, but he knew little about the church matter.

The party was to be in a new picnic area on the Han River. The class teacher made all the arrangements. It was a beautiful day for the outing. The class played games and sang songs, with everyone having a great time.

After Yong and Soon had eaten all they could, they sat down by the riverbank. The class was scattered, each with a friend, in the Korean custom, enjoying personal companionship when group activities were not in progress.

"Soon, I need to tell you something which is very personal to me. I feel you think I no longer want to be with you in the afternoons when I have to leave early. It's best I share with you something that happened last year."

Soon-sik knew his best friend had something important to tell and he just sat and listened without asking questions.

Yong continued. "After my grandmother died, I was sick in my heart. When I went to talk with Mr. Kim, my dear friend at our little store, I found I couldn't speak about the matter. But Mr. Kim came to me and told me how he had lost his family in a bad typhoon; his wife and their two daughters were killed. He said he found peace about their deaths after he went down to the church. That seemed strange to me.

"Mr. Kim asked me to go to church with him. That's how I

became enrolled in a Bible class. When I'm not with you or studying my school assignments, I'm reading and studying my Bible. I haven't found the answers to all my questions, but I feel in my heart that I'm on the right track."

The words tumbled out of Yong's mouth. He wanted to tell his dear friend for a long time, but did not have the opportunity until now. It was a load from his mind to be able to talk about such a personal matter with his friend.

Soon-sik did as most 12-year-olds who hear something they do not understand. He simply said, "Thanks, Yong, for sharing with me. I'd thought for a good while you didn't care for my company, that maybe you found a new friend. I guess you have in a way in Mr. Kim, but that's different. I hope you find what you want to know, and then you can tell me. It may be something everyone needs to know."

The matter was not mentioned between the two again. In the days ahead when Yong told Soon he had to leave early, he understood. At least he did not ask questions and he knew they were still friends. That was most important to both of them.

The life of Lee, Yong-soo fell into a routine. He attended school, spent some time with Soon-sik, excused himself, and headed for the corner to visit with his older friend. Then he would go home to begin his studies, which often lasted long into the night. Finally, even though exhausted, Yong would open his Bible to read a few lines from the book.

On Fridays Yong had his evening Bible class; on Sundays he would join the Sunday School class at church and worship with Mr. Kim. It was a busy life for a young man and time went by quickly.

Yong's life continued at a rapid pace. In the winter months, among his home chores, Yong had to be certain there was fuel in the home for his mother. After all, when his father was away, Yong was the man of the house. With this and the many subjects in school, days were short. Often he would finish his school assignments too exhausted to even open the Bible.

When the first sign of spring came, Yong rejoiced. He knew that summer meant a recess. He had attended most of the Bible classes, and they gave him real joy. Other things on his busy schedule had become quite a burden to him.

Summer finally came and classes were dismissed. Soon-sik spent the holidays visiting his grandparents in the country. Unlike summers of the past, there would be no loneliness for Yong when Soon was out of the city.

Yong began the summer by reporting to Mr. Kim the activities of the winter. He told of the many Fridays he had spent with his Bible teacher. He recalled the close friendship he had developed with Chang, Hee-sung, the most popular boy in the school. Mr. Kim noticed that Yong's life was revolving around the gift he had given him the previous summer. The Bible had become important to Yong.

"You're looking so refreshed today." Mr. Kim had taken in all Yong related and wanted him to know his good spirit was noticeable. "I've been thinking about a few things during this past year, and maybe it's time to share them with you."

It was almost as if he'd heard something like this before. He remembered how Mr. Kim had told about the special gift. His dear friend was about to say something important. Yong jerked up straight, listening intently.

Watching Yong's response, Mr. Kim knew he could speak freely. "Yong, it will be time for you to go to college in a few years. Your father will receive some help for your education through his work for the railway company, but college is very expensive these days. I was wondering if you would like to work for me in your spare time. We could study the Bible together when convenient. I'll tell your parents I'm putting the money you earn in a savings account to help with your education. You know I don't have a family now, and I want to help you with your career opportunities."

"Mr. Kim, you are full of surprises! I never know what you are thinking or what you're going to do next," replied Yong. "You're the most thoughtful man in the world! I don't care about the money, but I do want to come here and help each day. If you'll ask my parents for permission, I'm sure they'll give their approval."

This was the beginning of some wonderfully new and inspiring things for Yong. He could not know it at the time, but he was about to have his life changed for all eternity.

CHAPTER 8

A Personal Testimony

With agreement about the matter, and the promise of Mr. Kim to come to talk to his parents, Yong was off to tell his friend Hee-sung of the new development. Most of all, he wanted him to know about the opportunity to study the Bible each day.

Chang, Hee-sung was the most knowledgeable student in the Bible class and the most popular boy in Yong's school. The Chang family was not rich, but had a comfortable house and a yard larger than the Lees'. There was a fine wall around the house with a nice gate, which indicated that Mr. Chang's business was prospering. He sold paint and cleaning materials. When Yong ran into the yard, Hee's mother heard his footsteps and came to stand in the door.

Seeing Yong, she asked, "Well, Yong, what brings you breathless into our yard this afternoon? Is something wrong at your house?"

"No," replied Yong. "But I do need to see my friend. There are some personal matters I want to share with him. Is he here?"

"Yes, he's reading his Bible, but I'll call him." Mrs. Chang turned to call her eldest son to come and greet his visitor.

In a moment Chang, Hee-sung appeared at the door and welcomed Yong into the house. Hee's mother offered Yong some refreshment that was politely and humbly refused. Yong's desire to share the great news with his friend left him no time for other pleasures.

"Hee-sung," Yong began without any preparation or buildup to the subject, "I've just been offered the most wonderful opportunity by my friend Mr. Kim. He wants me to come to work for him this summer and use my extra time to help him during the school year. He's going to take the money and put it into a savings account for my education. Isn't that the greatest thing you've ever heard? Most important of all, we can study the Bible together when we are not busy."

All of this rolled off Yong's tongue. He had hardly taken a breath and his excitement was catching. "That's great, Yong!" Hee exclaimed.

When the excitement had worn off, the two sat down to enjoy the soft drink Hee's mother had brought into the room. She was a wise and good mother and knew both young men would appreciate a cool drink after their sharing had taken place.

It was then Chang, Hee-sung displayed the reason he was so popular in his school, so influential at church. The great moment of sharing had taken the two to a mountaintop of excitement. Hee thought it a good time to attend to another matter.

"Yong, you told me you began studying the Bible with Mr. Kim in an effort to find peace about the death of your grandmother. Well, there is something I'd like to discuss with you about that matter.

"You remember telling the Bible class, as we were discussing prayer, how your grandmother frequently had some beads she would hold in her hands. As she pulled the beads through her fingers, she would talk out loud. Then you told us that Pastor Choi and others talked out loud with their heads bowed when they were praying in church. Yong, you knew there was a difference, but you couldn't explain it. You didn't understand it. Is that right?"

There was something in the manner and tone of Chang, Hee-sung that Yong recognized. It was the same as when Mr. Kim was telling him about the Bible. He could hardly wait for Hee to continue and answered him softly, "Yes, Hee, I did say that, and it still concerns me. Can you help me?"

"Yes, in that and in another important matter. There is something you need to know. You have often felt that you could understand the words of the Bible, but not the real meaning. Isn't that true?"

Yong was startled. How could Hee or anyone else but Mr. Kim know about his personal feelings? Who told him? Curiosity about those questions caused Yong to reply softly, "Yes." His mind raced as he wondered where Hee-sung was leading and what he was sharing.

"What do you want to tell me?"

"I want to tell you about prayer and how you can learn the real meaning of the Scriptures," Hee replied. His younger friend was now listening intently, anxious for Hee to continue.

"Yong, when I was 12 years old, I had been going to church all of my life. My parents were Christians. I don't remember the first time I went to church. But at that early age I began to feel the need to pray. It was more than just wishing for something that I wanted. I felt a need to talk with God, but somehow I couldn't. I felt too dirty inside.

"When I wanted to pray, all those times I had disobeyed my parents and teachers came to my mind. I remembered those things which I had stolen in school that belonged to someone else, and the time I cheated on my exams. Yong, I was thinking of my personal sin and how much I've disappointed God. I just couldn't talk with God about it—I was ashamed."

"Why are you telling me these things?" Yong asked. He had never heard anyone talk like this in all of his life. Even Mr. Kim had not spoken of such personal things. His tone was serious, which led Hee-sung to continue.

"Well, Yong, for the first time Bible knowledge became something personal. I remembered what the pastor and my Bible teachers had taught me. They said Bible knowledge would remain in my head until it got into my heart. I didn't know what that meant. Yet I remembered how Jesus told Nicodemus that he had to be born again. I couldn't seem to understand that, but I wanted to be clean and able to come into God's presence.

"I had a yearning in my heart and remembered how Pastor Choi told us what to do when we wanted to pray truthfully for the first time. I got down on my face beside my pallet and asked Jesus Christ to come into my life. It was simple, truthful, and beautiful, Yong.

"You remember," Hee was rushing his words now, "we learned that Jesus died on the cross and shed His blood for our sins. Well, I knew He died for me, and it was my sin that caused Him to be on the cross."

Yong had heard about the death of Jesus many times in the months he had attended church and Bible class. He had joined a Sunday morning group of Bible students; and the teacher, along with Mr. Kim, had always taught the death of Jesus Christ for sinners. Not once had Yong thought or known this was personal. When Hee-sung told how he felt as a sinner, there was a rush of confusion to Yong's mind.

There were many questions Yong wanted to ask. His friend did not give him a chance to ask them. He had started now and he must finish. This was a personal testimony he had wanted to share with Yong for a long time.

"Yong, I had been taught that Jesus did not stay on that cross. We have studied many times how Jesus appeared to Mary and the others at the tomb. He made many other appearances, and even to the disciple Peter at the very last. Remember, it was Peter who had denied Jesus when those mean fellows wanted to kill him? Well, that made me think; if Jesus would forgive Peter, He would forgive me.

"I did a very personal thing. I asked Jesus Christ to forgive me, to come into my life, and be my Lord and Saviour."

Yong remembered the first time he heard the word *Lord.* It was the first Sunday he had visited the church with Mr. Kim. Now it was coming clear in his mind. Going to church or studying the Bible was not enough. Jesus had to become Lord, and somehow it seemed Chang, Hee-sung was showing him exactly how to make that happen.

"Well, how did you feel when you asked Jesus to clean you inside?" Yong was now eager to know the whole story.

"It was the most peaceful and clean feeling I've ever experienced in my life. I had to tell my parents, but I didn't know if they would understand it, even though they went to church regularly.

"When I told them, Mother cried and Father just bent low across his lap, holding his hands together with his eyes closed. He seemed to be thanking God. They told me they had been praying God would speak to my heart, that I would become a Christian. They had Pastor Choi come by the house. We talked and prayed together. He explained many things which I had questioned about Christianity. Then on Sunday it seemed everyone knew I had asked Jesus into my life."

It was time for Yong to reflect on all he'd heard. He knew Chang, Hee-sung was *different.* He had known that for a long time. He was stronger in character than the other classmates. Now it would seem God was showing Lee, Yong-soo how to be the same kind of person—different, but different with a purpose.

The final word from Chang, Hee-sung was so very personal that it could be passed only between close friends. Yong had known Hee was closer to him than any of the other older friends. Now it was certain. The sharing of this personal experience would mean the two would be friends for life.

The personal testimony of Hee's experience with Jesus Christ would never be forgotten. Yet the last personal remark was most challenging and instructive; it was memorable.

"Yong, you are my dearest friend. When you go home tonight, I want you to talk with Jesus. He needs to become your Lord too. It is time for you to become a Christian. Then you will understand about life and death."

This was the same thing Mr. Kim had said when Yong's grandmother had died. "When you become a Christian, you will be able to understand about life and death."

Yong made his way to the yard, giving a slight bow to Hee's mother as he said good-bye to the two of them. As he turned toward home, he realized he had two good friends who were interested in his well-being. He thought, Maybe both my friends are praying for me. It might be that I need to help God answer their prayers.

CHAPTER 9

A Glorious Experience

Yong's father had come home early, but the events of the day had given the young man so much to think about he hardly noticed either of his parents.

As he went to his supper, Yong was very quiet. His mother began to tell of her visit to Mr. Kim's store and their conversation. There was a new joy in her voice as she told of Mr. Kim's plan for her son.

Telling of the offer and the opportunity it presented, Yong's mother thought she would hear her son give an enthusiastic response. Instead, she was greatly puzzled, as was his father, at Yong's lack of enthusiasm.

It was a thoughtful and quiet son who asked to be excused from the table, having eaten little of his supper. The parents exchanged glances, wondering if Yong had gotten into some trouble he was keeping secret. It was one of those moments which causes tension to rise in a family, and Mother knew she would be the one who would address the situation.

Slipping into Yong's room, she was startled to see her son lying on his face on the floor. Rushing to him, she put her hand to his forehead to see if he was ill.

"Son, are you all right? You have been acting strangely since you came home. You showed no excitement about your new job and Mr. Kim's offer for your education. You did not eat much supper; you must be ill."

The questions came from the heart of one who loved her child. She had been his sole guardian for the many days that Yong's father was away at work. The excited observations of Yong's mother were so animated neither she nor Yong-soo noticed his father when he came to stand in the door.

"Son, did you hear your mother?" It was a tone of voice reserved for moments of correction. Yong's father seldom used it since his son had always been obedient to his parents.

The tension which had been building since Yong came home was now extreme. "Oh, sir, I am sorry," blurted Yong, seeing the distress on his father's face.

"Well, what is your explanation? You ate little of your mother's fine supper. You had little to say about my permission for you to have the job with Mr. Kim. It is not like you. What have you been doing that you are hiding from us?"

The remark gave Yong a start. He jumped from the floor and came to his father. "Sir, I am so sorry. I would not cause you or Mother any concern. I'm so happy Mr. Kim gave me the job, and I will be a good worker. When I went to my friend's house to tell him of my good fortune, he talked with me about a very serious matter. It filled my heart and mind, and I'm sorry I was not attentive at supper. Please forgive me."

Yong's parents were so relieved to hear their son was neither ill nor in serious trouble, they exchanged glances of relief and left his room without asking the nature of the talk with his friend Hee-sung.

As his parents left the room, Yong reached for his Bible. Turning to the Gospel of John, he began reading of Jesus' conversation with Nicodemus. It had been quite some time since his Bible class had studied that book of the Bible, but Yong remembered the questions Jesus answered in His encounter with Nicodemus.

Jesus told how to be born again. This was of great concern to Yong. He *had* to know what God wanted of him. He read the passage over and over again, searching the meaning of every word.

As he read, the words of Jesus concerning the Holy Spirit were meaningful to Yong. He had identified with Hee when his older friend told of his personal sins and his inability to pray sincerely. He thought of his own sin when Hee was reciting his failures.

"This is God's work in my heart," Yong was speaking in a soft, but audible, voice. With the thought came a deep desire to yield to God. Yong lowered his head and slowly stretched out on his face on the floor. He was now in a position of humble contrition to the One Who was speaking to his heart.

Yong stayed on his face in total silence. He never really knew when he began to speak to God in open prayer, for it was totally from the heart in spontaneous expression, which he had never known before this moment.

> Father God, I have read Your Word and know You sent Your Son, Jesus Christ, to die on the cross for me. I do not deserve life in Your kingdom.
>
> Today when Hee was speaking about lying, stealing, and cheating, You know how I felt in my heart, for You know my every thought and feeling. My mind has been filthy at times, and my heart is black with selfishness.
>
> Oh, Jesus, I want You to be my Lord. I believe Your death was for me, and Your blood will cleanse me of all my sin. Please come into my life and give me the presence of Your Holy Spirit. I will follow You and give You the first allegiance of my life.
>
> I will tell others about You with my life, my actions. Oh, thank You, Jesus. Oh, thank You for the warmth of Your presence. Oh, thank You for life. Thank You for making me one of Your children today!

Yong was not aware of time; he did not know how long he had been praying. The words came like a torrent of rain. He felt warm tears coming to his eyes. Only he and God knew the depth of feeling which had been building within him from the first day he had gone to church. Now the full bloom of the flower had come from the seed sown of that first hour of worship. It was God's flower, a new flower in His kingdom garden. It was a beautiful flower.

There was total peace in Yong's room. He lay on his back now, staring at the ceiling for the better part of an hour. He thought about the death of his grandmother and the friendship of Mr. Kim. He recalled how the pastor and the Bible teachers had been so faithful in their teaching. He knew he was blessed of God, and began speaking to Him in a prayer of thanks for the many blessings which were his in Jesus Christ. The visit to Hee-sung's home came to mind. Once again Yong was praying. This time it was silent, almost in a recital of all God had done for him.

These remembrances were mixed with a joy which made this the most glorious experience of his life. Yong was filled with the joy of the presence of God and he felt as if he could praise Him all night. There was great peace in his heart, and he remembered how Mr. Kim had spoken about such a peace concerning life and death when his grandmother had died. Too, it was the same which Chang, Hee-sung had shared.

As Yong's eyes came to rest on his Bible, he thought about Mr. Kim and the great times he would enjoy during recess. He wanted to go to the store right then to see if Mr. Kim was still there, but knew it was past a reasonable hour. Tomorrow would be soon enough.

Yong thought of his parents. How could he tell them of his glorious experience? They had never been to church. He had little he could share with them each week, as he knew they would never understand. This was a burden to his heart, but Yong decided to trust this matter to the Lord. He knew one day he could tell them all that was on his heart.

Rolling over on his pallet, Yong prayed. He held each of his parents before the loving Father Who had been so generous to him in his desire to understand about life and death. After all, he thought, if God can make me a Christian, He can bring my parents to know His love. I'll just pray for them, and I'm sure that one day they'll know God's love as I have come to know it tonight.

With that, Yong slipped off into the most peaceful sleep he had ever known. Little did he know that one day he would look back upon his experience with the knowledge that God had taken him by the hand for all that lay ahead.

CHAPTER 10

The World of the Christian

It was a different young man who sat down for breakfast with his parents on Sunday morning. He ate as if he were starved. His parents knew something had happened to him since he had been with them on Saturday night. They wondered if they needed to speak to him about his behavior.

Deciding it would be better to wait and give Yong time to tell them what they wanted to know, they asked no questions. When he finished his breakfast, he excused himself and prepared for church.

As he rushed from the house with a promise to be home after worship, Yong began singing the first song he had heard in church. It was "Amazing Grace." The difference today was Yong knew the meaning of the words. It was a reminder of the first time he went to church and would always be special to him.

When Mr. Kim saw Yong, he knew immediately there was something different about his young friend. He thought at first it must have been the offer of the job and the parents' consent. However, when they had walked only a short distance, Mr. Kim knew this was a different young man than he had known previously.

"Well, Yong," Mr. Kim began, "your parents were very easy to convince about the job for the recess. You should be proud of your family. They are very fine." It was just small talk. Mr. Kim knew Yong had something on his mind.

"Mr. Kim," Yong replied, "when you told me that someday I would know all about life and death, after Grandmother died, I doubted if I could ever know about that matter." It was as if Yong had not heard one word Mr. Kim had spoken. It was just as well, for Mr. Kim knew Yong had something important to share, and he was willing to hear him.

"Why do you mention that today, Yong?" he asked.

"Sir, yesterday I went to see my school friend Chang, Hee-sung to tell him of your offer of a job. While I was there, Hee told me about how he had become a Christian two years ago. He gave me a challenge about accepting Christ. I went home last night and did what Hee suggested. I talked with God in a very personal manner. It was the most peaceful and thrilling experience of my life. It is exactly as you told me. I asked Jesus to be my Lord; and when I went to sleep last night, I was filled with praises for God!"

Glancing up into Mr. Kim's face, Yong saw him wiping his cheeks with the clean handkerchief he always carried in his trouser pocket. Yong knew about the feeling, for it was the same as he had the night before; but one should not call attention to such when it occurs.

The expression on Mr. Kim's face told Yong the feeling his older friend had in that moment when Christ touched his heart. There were no adequate words to express it. The smile, the tears, and the actions expressed more than words could convey. Mr. Kim put his arm around his young friend. Yong remembered that strong arm because it had been around his shoulder the day he learned of his grandmother's death.

There was a squeeze on the shoulder as the two moved closer together. Now it was not intended, but man and boy walked in unison as they had never done before.

Just before they reached the church, Mr. Kim broke the holy silence of the walk by singing a hymn softly. It was "Amazing Grace," the song he heard Yong singing while coming down the hill. Both knew why they were singing. It was now "their song," and it marked a new era in the friendship of two whose hearts were inseparable in Christ's love.

As they came to the front of the church building and were about to part for their separate Bible classes, Mr. Kim spoke to Yong. He looked straight into his face and lowered his voice in a quiet and confidential tone.

"Son, I want you to know how proud I am of you today. I know you will be able to talk to your parents one day, but for now I want you to give me permission to speak to Pastor Choi. He will tell some others of your decision and then talk to you. One day he will baptize you. Do I have your permission to speak to him?"

"Of course!" Yong exclaimed with an enthusiastic tone that made Mr. Kim's heart leap. Yong started to leave, and turning, put his hand on his friend's arm and asked excitedly, "When do you think Pastor Choi will baptize me?"

"Oh, I don't know, but we will ask him after worship, and he will tell us," Mr. Kim said, turning once again to enter the building.

During Bible class, Yong-soo was attentive as never before. The teacher noticed his new enthusiasm, gave him some verses to read to the class, and asked him some special questions. Yong thought that he might inform the teacher and the class about his new decision, but hesitated because he thought they might not understand it. He would tell them later. This was difficult to keep to himself, and Yong wondered if he would always have trouble sharing it with others.

After Bible study, Yong rushed out to find Mr. Kim. They met in their usual place and went to take seats close to the front. Mr. Kim always sat near the front, telling Yong, "We'll leave the back seats for late arrivals." Yong knew that part of the reason was that his friend was getting just a little hard-of-hearing and needed to be near the front.

For nearly two years they had been together in worship. All of the people of Imja Dong Church knew Mr. Kim felt Yong was now a part of his family. Today it seemed there was a special radiance about the two of them as they sat waiting for worship to begin.

Yong remembered the first worship he had attended. He thought it was strange for people to talk with their eyes closed. He remembered how his grandmother did the same thing with her beads in her hands, but she didn't bow her head. He had learned since there was a difference.

In Christian worship there was genuine prayer to God Who encouraged His children to speak to Him. Yong was saddened to learn that talking to beads was not prayer, but a superstition many people practiced by worshiping gods made with hands, called idols.

Now Yong had no time for negative thoughts. He had a new joy and nothing could come to his mind that would take that joy from him.

When the choir began to sing, Yong was singing with them in his heart. He had once wondered why the people sang with such a glorious enthusiasm. Now he knew.

He had to stand on tiptoe to see the choir, but the effort was not a conscious one. Yong was as tall today as the tallest person in the whole church, if the feeling of the heart was the measure used.

It was a special sermon that Yong heard from Pastor Choi. He had thought often of Zacchaeus and how Jesus had gone home with him. The first sermon he heard was still in Yong's mind; it came to him that Jesus had gone home with him last night. In fact, Yong felt Jesus had come to church with him, in his heart, for His presence was so great!

The pastor spoke of a young woman who had come to a well on a hot summer day to draw some water. There she met Jesus Who asked her for a drink. The woman objected, as Jesus was a Jew. She said Jesus should not be speaking to her, for she came from another territory. The two groups of people lived in the same country, but were not on speaking terms.

Yong remembered the story, for it was in the Gospel of John, the first book he had studied in his Friday Bible class.

Pastor Choi spent most of his time talking about Jesus' answers to the woman's objections. One thing stuck in Yong's mind. Pastor Choi pointed out, "Jesus told the woman she could worship God anywhere, whether on a mountain or in the city of Jerusalem. God is spirit, and you can worship Him in spirit and truth anywhere you feel you want to reach out to Him from your heart."

That appealed to Yong. He knew he wanted to worship God every day in every place he went. He and Mr. Kim could worship in the store and pray together; he could worship in his room or when he was with Hee and other Christian friends; or when he was facing some problem in school. This was important for Yong to remember and he was very happy Pastor Choi had chosen the subject for his sermon.

Later, when Yong and Mr. Kim were greeting the pastor, and before one word could be spoken about Yong's decision, he told the pastor, "Sir, that is exactly what I needed to hear today. I thank you for showing me I can worship God every day in every place!"

Hearing that, Mr. Kim stepped forward to tell the pastor that Yong had asked Jesus Christ to come into his life the night before and needed to declare his profession of faith publicly for the Lord.

Pastor Choi leaned over and put both arms around Yong, surprising him greatly. "What a joy and delight you are, Yong!" the pastor exclaimed loudly. All those waiting to speak to the pastor heard the exclamation and knew what it meant.

"I knew you would settle the matter one of these days. Your Bible teachers have told me you were interested in becoming a Christian. Praise God for you! We'll have the joy of baptizing you," Pastor Choi almost shouted, so all could hear. It was a moment of joy for everyone present.

Yong was about to ask about baptism. He had seen a few others baptized in the time he had been coming to church. He looked up to Mr. Kim to give him an unspoken reminder he was to ask about it. Mr. Kim understood the reminder and asked, "Pastor, when do you think you will baptize Yong?"

"Well, sir, I think we can work it out in this manner. I will come by to visit Yong at the store tomorrow, since you have said he would be working for you. Then we will tell the leaders of the church. Next Sunday I will inform the people of Yong's decision, and by that time I should know the date for the baptismal service."

Reaching now to shake hands for a final good-bye, the pastor looked into Yong's face, asking, "My young Christian brother, how does that sound to you?"

Nods and thanks quickly confirmed the meeting, and the two friends stepped out the front door onto the sidewalk where many churchgoers were exchanging last-minute bits of news and information. By now word was around, and many people, including some Yong had never met, came up to shake hands and pat him on the back, congratulating him on his decision.

It was another quiet trip home. There was so much Yong wanted to talk about with Mr. Kim, but he knew they would be together every day for the next few weeks. There would be ample time for discussion and Bible study.

As they came to the hill on which the Lee home was located, Mr. Kim took Yong's hands and held them in his as he looked into the eyes of his young friend. Their eyes met. Not a word was spoken. This was a beautiful moment of reaffirmation for two who had known a glorious coming together in Jesus Christ. Their spirits were now one with Him and one another. The difference in age and experience mattered little in this moment of deep reflection by two who had come to be one in the Lord.

Slowly they broke the grip and Yong started to leave. Before he turned toward his home, Mr. Kim stood looking as Yong was making his way up the hill.

He stopped Yong in his tracks with, "Yong, I have something special I want to share with you tomorrow. You will enjoy it, and when we have time I will show it to you. You remember I have two books on my table at the store. It is time, since you are going to live in the world of a Christian, for me to share the second book with you. We'll read it together as we have time during your holidays."

As Yong climbed the hill, he thought, Well, he's done it again. I just can't get ahead of Mr. Kim. He's always thinking about me; how he can help me. When I grow up, I want to help people just as he's helped me. I haven't thought about that second book for many months. I wonder why it's so important. But if Mr. Kim wants us to read it, then it must be something special. This should be a wonderful summer recess.

Yong had been a Christian less than 24 hours, but he knew beyond all doubt it was to be a life much different than he had ever thought. It was wonderful to be a citizen of the kingdom of Christ.

CHAPTER 11

Meeting Pilgrim

Summer recess for Yong was a time when life seemed to be one continuous experience of God's grace. Unlike days of past summers, Yong was out of bed, dressed, and waiting for his mother to finish breakfast.

Yong's father, preparing to leave for the week, knew something had happened to his son. When he had more time, he would talk to Yong about church business and changes he saw taking place.

At the same time, Yong was praying each morning God would show him how to share his new experience with his parents. He wanted them to attend church with him, but had been so concerned about matters he could not understand himself, he had little time to think about his parents. Now it was different, and he wanted to tell both of them about Jesus and His love for them.

Yong knew God would show him how to tell them, but for now he had to get down to the store, for Mr. Kim wanted him on the job early.

The shopkeeper knew his young friend was excited about his new job, for Yong was at the store when he arrived.

Yong greeted Mr. Kim loudly and happily, saying, "Good morning, Mr. Kim; I arrived earlier than you today. You know how much I appreciate the opportunity to work for you this summer."

"Good morning, Yong. It is good you're eager and have come early for we have much to do today."

As he spoke, Mr. Kim reached for his store keys. Removing the metal protective coverings from the door which kept his store safe from thieves, he looked at his young friend to see the changes he could notice in him. He was aware, as was Yong's father, this was a different young friend than he had known previously; but, unlike Mr. Lee, he knew the reason.

"Yesterday was a great day," Mr. Kim spoke slowly, as if he were about to make an observation. Yong was familiar with the tone and knew something important was coming.

"Yes, sir, it was a great day; one I'll never forget."

"Well, we must talk about it. You see, son, we don't spend every day in church. We have to meet the world, and that means we must be able to tell each person we meet about Christ."

This startled Yong. "You mean we have to stop and tell each customer who comes into the store about Jesus?"

In the same serious tone, Mr. Kim replied, "Yes, in a manner of speaking, that is exactly what I mean. But, Yong, we don't have to stop what we are doing and speak to them personally; we have to tell them by the way we treat them, how we listen to what they tell us. There are those whom the Lord sends our way whom we tell personally. Most people, however, receive our witness by looking at us, hearing how we speak, and watching how we take interest in them."

A light came on in Yong's mind, and a broad smile, seemingly of relief, came across his face. Quickly he replied, "Oh, is *that* what you mean?"

"Yong, it's not easy being honest and sincere; making people feel comfortable; refraining from being critical of them when you learn their faults; loving them in spite of how much they gossip and speak ill of others. It may sound simple and unimportant, but that's the way we tell others about Jesus. When they see us treating them as persons of worth, they know there is something different about us. We must let them see Jesus when they look at what we are doing for them. That way the Lord receives the glory and credit, and we are His instruments."

All of this conversation took place while Mr. Kim was preparing for the day's work: counting the money he had taken from his pocket before putting it in the money box; dusting and cleaning the weekend dirt from the merchandise. Yong had followed his lead and began to sweep the store before the first customer came.

He was about to finish that chore when a young customer, about two years younger than Yong, came to purchase a box of cookies. It was the first time Yong had seen the young man.

As he waited on the younger man, he recalled how much had happened to him since his first trip to Mr. Kim's shop. He received a new and warm feeling just thinking about it. His impulse was to tell this customer, and every customer that day, of his glorious experience, but time and prudence would not permit it.

The truck with the new stock, which arrived early each Monday, stopped at the front of the store. All serious conversation was over for a while, and it was just as well. Yong knew that Mr. Kim's idea about telling the world about Jesus was more than following impulse, it was something he had to think about before he could understand all of it.

Monday was a busy morning, and before the two could stop and talk about personal matters, Pastor Choi arrived. Earlier in the morning, Yong's friend Hee-sung had dropped by with a word of praise for the news he had heard about the activities of the previous day. Yong felt the new interest Hee had in him was one of those things which made life so much better these days.

Pastor Choi was a busy man. He took a few minutes to speak about some church matters with Mr. Kim; then asked permission to speak privately with Yong-soo.

The two went to the little table at the rear of the store. Pastor Choi opened the Bible and began to review the matter of how one becomes a Christian. He reassured himself that Yong had sincerely asked Jesus Christ into his life by asking a few very direct questions, to which Yong gave clear and concise answers.

Having satisfied himself about Yong's Christian experience, he took his calendar booklet from his coat pocket. "Yong, we will baptize you on a Sunday evening in our church. You have seen these services, I'm sure, but I'll ask you to come to my study in the church. At that time, I'll explain the meaning of baptism and how we'll proceed."

The two agreed on a date a few weeks ahead. Then the young Christian received a challenge from his pastor.

"Yong, I am satisfied that Mr. Kim will teach you how to share Christ with those you meet here in the store. Too, you must learn how to tell your classmates and friends about Jesus. This won't be easy; but in order to do that, you must be faithful in your Bible study and personal prayertime. Take every advantage of all we do to help you grow as a Christian with our special classes at church."

Yong wanted to tell his pastor of the earlier conversation he had with Mr. Kim about the same matter, but was not given a chance. He decided to listen carefully and make the best impression possible.

The pastor asked if Yong had any questions and prepared to leave for his next appointment. He finished the soft drink Mr. Kim had placed on the table and walked to the door. Yong asked him if he could make a statement and received a nod of the head with, "Certainly."

"Pastor, we have many friends in our school and in our community who are not Christians. Many of them come into the store. We need to help them learn of our Christ. Too, my parents need to know my Lord. I want to be the kind of Christian who will help God reach each one of these with His love. Too, I want your prayers for my parents."

These words rolled off Yong's tongue as if they had been rehearsed. It was a sincere statement and indicated a kind of maturity in the young Christian which Pastor Choi did not expect.

The pastor responded by praising Yong for his high desires. He reminded him of the arrangements about the baptism. He then left as quickly as he had come.

Mr. Kim was deeply impressed, and said as much. As he spoke of his impressions, he made his way to his chair to rest for a moment.

The two had earlier prepared their noon meal on Mr. Kim's small stove he had in the store. He used it for many things, including preparing squid, to the delight of his younger customers. On this day, however, the two did not get to eat until midafternoon because of interruptions.

As the afternoon lull came, it gave Yong time to eat and think about Mr. Kim's promise of the previous day.

"Oh, sir," Yong almost blurted the words as the thought came to his mind about the promise, "you have something you wanted to share with me today. We've been so busy I almost forgot it."

"I didn't forget, Yong, but this is a good time of the day to begin. It'll take us a few days to complete what I have in mind. Take your chair and we'll begin."

As Mr. Kim spoke, he reached into his shirt pocket, taking out his glasses. Yong knew he was about to read. He thought it might be some special passage from the Bible.

When Mr. Kim reached under the table and brought out the second book, Yong was surprised. He had forgotten about the second book.

"Yong, this is an excellent book for a Christian to read. It was written by an Englishman, John Bunyan, who was in a Bedford, England, prison for preaching the gospel without permission. In those days there was no freedom to read and interpret the Bible as we do today.

"This book was first published a few years before his death in

1688. It has become a Christian classic. The book is *The Pilgrim's Progress."*

Mr. Kim then explained the book was an allegory, which meant the story and the names were used to describe something else. In this book the story was about the life of a Christian and the many kinds of people and trials one would meet on the journey toward heaven, which Mr. Bunyan called Celestial City. The Christian was first given the name Pilgrim, indicating one who was on a journey into territory he had never seen.

Mr. Kim's explanation came so easily and clearly; Yong was overwhelmed. Yet he was puzzled why such an old book, written 300 years ago, could be important today. The wise old Christian saw the look on Yong's face and understood.

"You want to know why I would think such an old book is important to those of us today, don't you?

"Well, it *is* a very old book; one should wonder about how useful it would be today." He spoke softly, for he didn't wish to show offense; yet Mr. Kim had startled him by reading his mind.

"Yong-soo, this is about a man in prison who has a dream. He sees one who desires to become a Christian. The pilgrim leaves his home and starts his journey. It reveals the difficulties and the victories one who is a seeker may have in becoming a Christian and living that life each day."

Pausing for a moment to let his words sink into Yong's heart, Mr. Kim continued his presentation. "It is the story of the journey you are about to take, Yong, what you will face and how you'll be able to overcome the obstacles in your life for Christ. In some sense we're all Christian pilgrims. That's why I want to read this book with you. We'll take the time to explain those things you don't understand. It should be a good experience for both of us."

With that, Mr. Kim opened the old and worn book. He read the opening words of the author with his lengthy "The Author's Apology." It sounded strange to Yong that an author would apologize for the book he had written; he wondered aloud about it.

Mr. Kim explained this was the author's way of revealing his humility at undertaking such an important subject. He had to prove to the reader he was not the final authority on such matters. In fact, the older Christian explained, it revealed the true spirit of the man.

"Maybe that's the reason the book is still being read," he said.

During the days that followed, the shopkeeper and his young friend were together at the table constantly, when not interrupted or doing things which had to be done.

Mr. Kim was a good reader. He would take the time to explain the allegorical meanings of the characters and events, making the book extremely interesting to his young listener.

The regular customers became accustomed to seeing the two reading the book, or in conversation with one another on a subject which seemed to be personal. At times the two were so involved customers had to wait for some explanation or discussion to end before they could receive service.

It mattered little. The older customers had seen Yong around the store since early childhood. They knew he belonged, and accepted the relationship as something good for the old man and his young friend.

For Yong it was a wonderful summer. As they read, he was able to follow Christian on his pilgrim's journey. He learned the meaning of many new words, and Mr. Kim had an opportunity to teach him about the varied personalities he would meet in life. Most importantly, he could point out the difficulties a Christian encountered in life. This was the purpose Mr. Kim had in mind when he suggested they read the book together.

Yong took a deep interest in the episode where Pilgrim had to go through the Slough of Despond. Yong began to identify with the story at this point.

"Pilgrim's family did not want him to make the journey, but he persisted, Mr. Kim."

"That's right, son, and what does that tell you?"

"Well, my family is not Christian. The only religion they've ever known has been Buddhism. Since Grandmother's death, they've encouraged me to go to church. They don't know what's happened to me, and in some ways I feel like Pilgrim."

Mr. Kim put his hand to his chin, staring at the floor. "Yong, there will be other things you'll learn from this story. That's why we're reading it. Pilgrim had a heavy burden in the early days of his journey!"

Yong was so elated with his Christian life, he had forgotten the times his heart felt heavy as to his own condition, when he couldn't grasp or understand much that he read in the Bible.

When he mentioned this to Mr. Kim, he added, "Yes, and too, your new joy has made you forget you carried a burden about your own sins before God. You must never forget life will not always be as beautiful as it has been for you recently.

"Listen carefully to how Mr. Bunyan describes Christian's journey from the City of Destruction to Mount Zion. Notice how many people tried to hinder the journey; and note those who helped."

Yong remembered reading that one great helper to the pilgrim was the Interpreter. He had his own Interpreter. One day he would tell his friends, "No young man ever has had as wise and gentle a Christian friend as Mr. Kim."

Late one afternoon the two read of the Christian and the cross. He had Mr. Kim mark the passage, so he could find it in the future, so he could read it to others.

> Now I saw in my Dream, that the highway up which Christian was to go, was fenced on either side with a Wall, and that Wall was called Salvation. Up this way therefore did burdened Christian run, but not without great difficulty, because of the load on his back.
>
> He ran thus till he came at a place somewhat ascending, and upon that place stood a Cross, and a little below in the bottom, a Sepulchre. So I saw in my Dream, that just as Christian came up with the Cross, his Burden loosed from off his shoulders, and fell from off his back, and began to tumble, and so continued to do, till it came to the mouth of the Sepulchre, where it fell in, and I saw it no more.
>
> Then was Christian glad and lightsome, and said with a merry heart, He had given me rest by his sorrow, and life by his death. Then he stood still awhile to look and wonder; for it was very surprising to him, that the sight of the Cross should thus ease him of his Burden. He looked therefore, and looked again, even till the springs that were in his head sent the waters down his cheeks.

Later Yong was to see the further difficulties of the Christian. None were so clear as the meeting he had with Apollyon, the type of Satan. It was here Mr. Kim took great pains to explain that every Christian would meet Satan, and the armor God provides is the only protection one has at that time. In fact, Mr. Kim told Yong, "In some way each day you will have to battle Satan."

This did not frighten Yong, for Mr. Kim assured him, "Satan has already lost the war; now he wants to win the daily battles. But one must remember God says, 'He who lives within the Christian is greater than the one who reigns in the world.'"

As they finished the book, Mr. Kim reviewed it with his young clerk. "Yong, never forget the places Christian visited on his way to Mount Zion and Celestial City. You'll have your Hill Difficulty, Valley of the Shadow of Death, and Dungeon of Despair, as did John Bunyan's Christian, before you complete your journey. Remember the people you'll meet, like Formalist, Hypocrisy, and Hopeful, will be real people. They'll need your help. Never forget,

Hopeful saw all Christian encountered. It gave him the desire to become a Christian. That's why we have trials. God uses them for His glory."

The time spent with work and reading made the summer weeks pass quickly. Yong spent most of his time at the store and saw little of friends or family.

Mr. Kim remembered the new things he had been able to teach Yong during the summer. They had grown closer as brothers in Jesus Christ. Both had rejoiced in the conclusion of the book, with the note of victory for Christian.

The final word Mr. Kim gave about the subject was short and simple. "No one can face your trials for you. You are not going to be exempt from difficulties. You can talk to your pastor, your friends, or to me, but most of all you can talk to our Lord when your burden gets too heavy."

These were prophetic words for Yong, though he did not know it when he heard them. After all, the summer of his first year as a Christian had been with his best friend. He had been able to save money for college, and, at the same time, read a great adventure story about a Christian. There was nothing more a young man could desire. God was certainly good! He would remember this summer for the remainder of his life. Little did he know how it would shape his character for the days ahead.

CHAPTER 12

The Valley of the Shadows

A few days after the new school term began, Yong attended the Friday evening Bible class. Pastor Choi came by and asked if he could speak to Yong.

The pastor received the teacher's permission, and Yong stepped to the door to meet him. "Greetings, Yong. I talked with your friend Mr. Kim yesterday. He says you are anxious to be baptized. Well, I have some plans to share with you."

Yong's heart leaped. "Yes, sir, I'm excited about the baptismal service. Please tell me your plans."

"Yong, I'm interested in having your parents attend your baptism. What do you think about my stopping by tomorrow and speaking to them?" The pastor knew he didn't need Yong's permission, but thought it was the right thing to share with this new Christian.

"Oh, that will be great, sir!" This was an answer to Yong's prayer. He had prayed earnestly for God to show him a way to speak to his parents. He mentioned to them he would be baptized, but neither had responded, as they did not understand much that Yong told them about the matter.

"I'll invite them to come, and have Mr. Kim stop by to bring them, as he did you. We'll have the service on a Sunday evening. I know your father leaves for work on Sunday afternoons, but Mr. Kim thinks he will stay over for such an important event in your life."

The pastor's remarks indicated to Yong everything had been thought out thoroughly. He was convinced of this when the pastor said, "Yong, take your Bible and read of the baptism of Jesus. Then read about Jesus' Resurrection. Tomorrow afternoon at 3:00 we'll meet in my office here at the church. We'll discuss these matters, and I should know your parents' response by that time."

The conversation ended with Yong's nod of understanding. They gave each other a slight bow, and Yong went back into class. His friends wondered what the pastor wanted with Yong. He answered their unspoken questions as he whispered to one of his classmates, "The pastor told me about the arrangements for my baptism. He's going to invite my parents!"

The next day, as the family was finishing their noon meal, a familiar voice was heard in the Lees' yard. "Mr. Lee, can I come in? I need a few words with you and your fine wife."

Yong recognized Pastor Choi's voice, and said quietly to his mother, "It's my pastor." With a quizzical glance at his wife, Yong's father went to the door.

"Come in, Pastor Choi. I've heard Yong speak of you often. We feel as though we've met you. We hear your words repeated frequently here in our home. Yong says you are the best pastor in all of Imja Dong."

This warm greeting by Mr. Lee made Pastor Choi's reason for the visit easier to approach. "Well, you have a fine son, and both of you should be proud of him. We have watched him in these last several months, and he is making a good Christian."

Both parents exchanged glances of pride; smiles of appreciation crossed their faces. "Thank you, Pastor. You know, when Yong's grandmother died, Mr. Kim was a great help to us. Our son felt so bad about the death; we didn't know what to tell him. When Mr. Kim took him to church, well, things began to change. I can't explain it, but I'm sure you know all about it."

Pastor Choi was ready for this and said, "Yes, I know about it and that's why I'm here today. Yong has become a Christian. It's time I baptize him. Mr. Kim and I have discussed the matter and we want the two of you to be present for the occasion. He says he will come for you. We are planning it for one week from tomorrow night. We know you leave on Sunday afternoons for work, but thought maybe you would stay over for the baptism. It'll mean much to Yong-soo."

Without hesitation, Mr. Lee nodded his head as he looked at Yong. "Why, of course we'll be there. It was kind of you, Pastor, to come give us a personal invitation. Tell Mr. Kim we'll appreciate his coming for us. We'll be ready if he tells us the time he's coming."

The pastor seemed to enjoy the coffee and cookies Yong's mother hastily brought from her kitchen. No proper Korean hostess would let a guest leave without refreshments.

The four discussed many of the matters of general interest about Korea and Imja Dong. Yong was impressed as to the ease with which Pastor Choi and his parents related. One would have thought they were old friends.

Possibly, thought Yong, my many references to church and Pastor Choi have made my parents aware of how great it is to be Christians.

Reminding Yong they had an appointment later in the day, Pastor Choi excused himself, thanking the Lees for their hospitality.

As soon as Pastor Choi was out of hearing distance, Mr. Lee asked Yong if he had invited the pastor to the home.

"If you did, why didn't you tell us beforehand?" This took Yong by surprise. It was not a harsh tone his father used, but one which indicated he would not appreciate it if Yong had set this appointment without telling them about it.

"No, Father, I did not invite Pastor Choi. He came by the Bible class last night and told me he was going to invite the two of you to the baptism. I told him that would be great, but he did not ask me to inform you or tell me when he would be coming here. But I'm glad he came, aren't you?"

That brought a smile to his father's face. "Yes, I'm glad he came. We've wanted to meet him since the first day you went to church. He seems to be a fine gentleman. We're happy he and Mr. Kim have taken an interest in you. We'll attend the baptismal service."

The pastor and Yong met as scheduled. The study was thorough as to the reason Jesus was baptized; what it related to in His life; and how it symbolized His death, burial, and Resurrection. Yong was with the pastor nearly two hours.

The next days were filled with much anticipation. Yong and Mr. Kim often discussed the significance of the events of the last several months.

As was planned, the Lees attended Yong's baptism. They met many of those whom Yong had mentioned; among those were his Bible class and Sunday School teachers, his older friend Chang, Hee-sung, and others that were spoken of in the home.

Mr. Kim had done for them what he had done for Yong. He escorted them to church, explained what was happening, and introduced them to Yong's friends. It was a great and meaningful event.

Mr. Lee remarked how he was glad he'd stayed over and Pastor Choi had come to give them an invitation.

The next days and months slipped by quickly for Yong. He helped Mr. Kim at every opportunity; spent time with his friend Cho, Soon-sik, who began attending the Friday Bible class; studied harder than ever, with the idea of preparation for college on his mind; and assisted his mother with home affairs. He noticed his father's absence became a greater burden to his mother since Grandmother was gone.

Several months passed, when one afternoon, Yong-soo and his friend Cho, Soon-sik had some time to be together. They decided to walk toward the Han River. They did this frequently in times past, but it was seldom the two could get away to visit their favorite place nowadays.

Soon-sik was interested in becoming a Christian. He had planned many times to talk with Yong. This was his opportunity.

It was the month of Yong's 18th birthday. The festival of Chusok, the Korean season of thanksgiving and family gatherings, was on the minds of everyone. Prosperity had come to many; and new automobiles filled the streets, whizzing by the two as they walked along the Han River road. They were unmindful of the rushing traffic, consumed in the idea that Soon-sik wanted some answers to questions about being a Christian.

Yong and Soon had been friends since the first days of elementary school. They wondered aloud at times what would happen if they did not have one another to share their joys and sorrows with each day. One of the favorite places for this sharing in days past was the bank of the old Han River. It was to this place they walked instinctively.

As the two sat watching the recently widened and beautified river flowing slowly to a destination all its own, Soon-sik spoke about his own spiritual destination. It was here, as the afternoon sun eased slowly behind the southern ridge of mountains, that Yong-soo did for Soon-sik what his older friend Chang, Hee-sung had done for him many months ago. He told him how to repent and ask Jesus Christ into his life. They discussed Bible passages on the new birth, which they had studied in the Friday Bible class.

Soon-sik thought Yong was looking into his mind when his Christian friend said, "Soon, I know you have thought many times about all of this. You've wondered why you couldn't find the answer. It is not a matter of knowledge; it is of faith. You need to go home, get alone, and do what each one of us has had to do—ask

Jesus Christ to come into your life. Then you'll have the answers. That's the only way."

Neither of the two noticed that darkness had slowly covered the river and their favorite talking place. They were so consumed with Soon-sik's needs and how to meet them that time had passed rapidly.

They had told their parents they were going to take a walk to the river, but neither thought they would be out past sunset. Now they needed to hurry home.

As they walked, the conversation continued. Soon-sik asked questions he had thought about for many months. Yong's answers were clear and simple.

The two stepped out into the river road, walking shoulder to shoulder. Traffic now seemed faster than in the afternoon; and as they walked in the street, the two would stop from time to time to permit cars to pass without having to move into another lane because of their presence.

Yong never saw the car that hit him. He felt himself flying through the air; lights whirled about him in a blur. Then blackness . . . total blackness!

Soon-sik saw the taxi and stepped from its path. He did not have a moment to warn his friend.

The taxi driver braked to a stop at a right angle to the street curb. He threw open his door and came quickly to assist Yong. The victim's head rested on top of the curb, and his body pointed toward the river. The crazy pattern from the taxi's headlights made eerie shadows dance across the scene.

The driver mumbled about not seeing Yong, or something about the foolish boy being in the street. His hands shook as he reached down to the limp form. He wanted to help Yong, but couldn't; fright sapped his strength. He was helpless to assist the helpless.

Soon-sik kneeled over Yong, calling his name. He received no reply. In that moment a big hand reached over Soon-sik's shoulder. A truck driver following closely behind the taxi had seen the young man fly through the air. He had come to take him to the hospital, if he could.

Many curious bystanders gathered in a knot around Yong, thinking the helpless victim was dead. In hushed tones, they asked unanswerable questions and made meaningless statements.

Years of experience on the highways told the truck driver he must take charge. He moved the crowd back with a stern voice as he scooped Yong into his arms. A life so full and vibrant a moment ago now seemed to be in its last minutes. Arms and legs hung lifeless and limp. Yong's head, cradled against the huge breast that held it, was a mass of blood.

"Let's take him to the hospital in my car. There's one near here." The voice came from a well-dressed man whose car was at the curb a few feet in front of the taxi. His was a voice of authority, and the truck driver started to the automobile with his precious burden.

He had to wait a moment before placing Yong on the back seat, for the owner had rushed ahead. He was talking on his car telephone. Soon-sik heard him shout, "We're bringing in an accident victim, and we're not far from you."

Soon-sik identified himself to the car's owner as Yong's friend. He reached out and pulled Soon into the front seat with him. As he closed the door, he glanced over his shoulder to see if there was any sign of life. All he could see by the overhead car light was a blood-covered, unconscious form. He couldn't tell whether Yong was breathing.

The owner said, "It's good I was a patient in this hospital earlier this year. That's how I knew the number to call. It's close, and they do good work." Soon thought this was a fortunate coincidence; later he would know it was a miracle of God.

The chauffeur made the trip to the hospital quickly and without incident. The three never spoke a word, except for Soon to say, "I hope he lives. O God, please let him live." If the other two heard him make this remark, they did not respond.

Arriving at the hospital, the driver wheeled the car around to the emergency room entrance. Three nurses and an orderly were waiting and rolled a stretcher to the car. With great care they eased Yong onto it and moved swiftly to the emergency room.

Soon-sik and his two nameless companions followed the stretcher. The car owner and his driver stopped at the reception desk; Soon went with Yong. He moved now as if nothing were real. He knew this couldn't be happening to him. One moment he was thinking about becoming a Christian, and the next he was standing over his buddy who looked like he was dead.

When the nurse yelled, "I've got a pulse!" Soon came back to reality. The duty doctor mumbled something like, "We'll be lucky to save this one. Looks like he's got a fractured skull, among other things."

With that he began barking orders like an army drill sergeant. Nurses rushed around Yong giving injections and monitoring his pulse. One remarked that it was weak and she could barely find it. Another put a wrap on his arm, which Soon knew to be a blood pressure measuring device. He saw her check it several times, shaking her head. Then she yelled, "Oxygen!"

Soon's mind had not been functioning well. He tried to reconstruct the tragic event. He was jarred from this, however, when a nurse asked him if he knew the patient's name and parents.

Yong's clothes had been cut from him when he was brought into the emergency room. Soon saw them on the floor, slick with blood. He picked up what was left of Yong's trousers to get his identification holder from one of his pockets. Soon thought he was going to faint.

The nurse noticed the change in Soon's complexion and asked him to step outside with her. The man in the business suit and the driver stepped forward to ask if Yong was still alive. When they heard the reply, "Yes, right *now,*" they gave the nurse their names and excused themselves. Soon didn't take the opportunity to thank them; they didn't seem to expect it; they showed only great relief that Yong was still alive.

Soon needed to make a telephone call; he had to notify Mr. Kim. He remembered the number at the store, since he had called Yong there many times. He asked to use the reception desk phone and dialed the number. When Mr. Kim answered, Soon told him of the tragic events of the last few minutes.

"Mr. Kim, Yong looks like he might die. Can you notify Mrs. Lee and Pastor Choi?" Mr. Kim asked for the address of the hospital and the telephone number. As he hung up, Soon-sik heard Mr. Kim say something about "the valley of the shadow of death." He had heard those words before, but he wondered why Mr. Kim repeated them right now.

CHAPTER 13

When All Things Work Together

The next 30 minutes were the longest and most meaningful that Cho, Soon-sik had ever experienced. He turned to go back into the emergency room when the nurse stopped him with, "It is better now that you remain outside."

That was enough for Soon-sik. He had mixed emotions. He wanted to be with his friend, but the sight and smell of the emergency room were too much for him.

As he sat waiting for family and friends to arrive, Soon thought back to the reason for the meeting with Lee, Yong-soo. He had wanted to talk about becoming a Christian.

In that moment Soon made a life-changing decision. He knew he did not have to wait until the quiet of his home to talk to Jesus. If there was ever a time when he needed the Lord, it was at this moment.

Tears moved slowly down his cheeks. He thought of his friend on the table in the adjoining room. The need of his own heart became clear. It was as if Jesus were standing before him saying, "You can come to me now, Cho, Soon-sik, if you open your heart."

Soon lowered his head, closed his eyes. In silence he began the same kind of prayer Yong-soo had prayed in his room. It was a simple, quiet admission of sin, the desire to have Jesus Christ in his life and the request for forgiveness which Soon uttered in total silence.

Later, when he shared this with Pastor Choi requesting baptism, he told how he had yielded to the lordship of Jesus Christ. He told of the peace that came to his heart in his moment of submission.

He said, "I sat down in the waiting room with great fear about my friend. I came, however, to a complete understanding about my own future in Christ Jesus. Then I received peace about myself and about Yong. It was almost too good. One moment, total panic; the next, total peace."

Soon's personal moment with the Lord was interrupted by a hand on his shoulder. He was startled as someone asked, "Soon, where is Yong-soo? Can I see him?" It was Mr. Kim. He had notified those whom Soon had mentioned on the telephone, quickly closed his store, and taken a taxi straight to the hospital.

"Oh, Mr. Kim, I'm so glad to see you!" Soon reached out to embrace the shopkeeper. Mr. Kim noticed the wet cheeks of his young friend and thought how deeply Soon cared for Yong-soo.

"Yong's in the emergency room, Mr. Kim. I don't know if he'll make it. He's hurt badly. I believe the doctor said something about a fractured skull." The quick words and thoughts created some confusion in Mr. Kim's mind.

"Wait a minute, son. Tell me if I can see Yong."

Soon took his older friend by the arm and stepped toward the door to the room where Yong was being treated. They were both startled, for in that moment the door opened. The nurses were moving Yong on the rolling table into the waiting room.

"How is he? Where are you taking him?" The questions were almost rhetorical; Mr. Kim did not give anyone a chance to answer.

The blood and intravenous fluid bags were hanging from long steel poles fastened to the rolling cart. The nurses were busy keeping the bags, their plastic tubes, and Yong's oxygen mask in place. One was struggling with the portable oxygen tank. They did not have time to answer specific questions.

"We are taking him to radiology. We can't tell how badly he's hurt until we get some pictures. The doctor thinks he's got some fractures, but we can't confirm that until we get pictures. Too, he's got some broken ribs, and we hope there's no internal damage. We're doing all we can. Just keep the family here, and the doctor will inform you as soon as he can determine the damage."

As the nurses spoke, they made their way to the elevator. It was matter-of-fact information; nothing personal, no emotion. They did this every day and made it seem routine.

To the two who heard it, there was nothing routine about it. They were hearing about one they loved. Soon's love was for a lifetime friend, and his fear was of losing him forever. Mr. Kim's love was for a little fellow he had known all of his life, one who was now his brother in Jesus Christ. His was not a fear, but a deep longing for God to let the young man live that he would be able to continue to witness of the glory of the Lord.

Soon and Mr. Kim had the same thought. The elevator door closed; they turned to each other. Mr. Kim spoke first. "Soon, it's time to pray. Let's sit on this bench. We need to talk to the Lord about Yong-soo."

Soon nodded, and they moved together to a bench along one wall of the waiting room. As they sat down, Soon spoke. "Mr. Kim, I must tell you something very important. A few moments ago, I knew I needed to talk to God about Yong. I remembered that Christians are the ones who can truly talk to God. This afternoon Yong-soo told me how to become a Christian. I was on my way home to consider his suggestions when the taxi hit him. So a few moments ago, I asked Jesus Christ to come into my life. And He did!"

There was hardly time for Mr. Kim to respond. He reached over, took Soon's arm in his strong hand, and squeezed it. A warm and gentle look crossed Mr. Kim's face; it was fleeting, but Soon saw it. That confirmation was all Soon needed.

Mr. Kim bowed his head and began praying aloud in a soft voice, as if he were talking to an old friend:

> Father, we are Yours. You have redeemed us. You know the reason for our being here. We have our friend Lee, Yong-soo on our hearts. He is hurting. We ask You to touch his body, spare his life, so that he may continue to be Your witness. We know Yours is the greater wisdom. We yield to that for Yong's life and ours. And thus we pray, "Nevertheless, not my will but Thine be done."
>
> Accept our thanks for Soon's salvation. May Your Spirit guide him all the days of his life.
>
> Lord Christ, please intercede for Yong. We love You and ask this in Your precious and healing name. Amen.

As they lifted their heads, Mrs. Lee came through the door. Pastor Choi was by her side, the two having met outside the hospital.

"Oh, Mr. Kim, how is Yong? Is he still alive? Where is he? May I see him?" The torrent of questions came with an unnaturally high pitch; fear and anxiety had overtaken Yong's mother.

"Mrs. Lee," Mr. Kim began, with a very steady and controlled voice in an attempt to calm her, "we saw the nurses take Yong to radiology a few moments ago. Yes, he's alive. It would seem since they are able to move him, his condition has stabilized somewhat. They want to determine the extent of his injuries. That's all they'll tell us. In cases like these, which they see here every day, it would seem they get some preliminary answers rather soon. Then, if all goes well, we'll know the total damages later."

Mr. Kim's words were like oil on water which had been troubled by disaster. It was as if someone great, some presence, inspired him. It was calming and assuring.

Pastor Choi had been satisfied for Mrs. Lee to ask the questions. He spoke quietly now to Mr. Kim. The two were in personal conversation. Cho, Soon-sik had been listening intently to Mr. Kim's remarks. He knew the pastor was asking if Mr. Kim knew anything he was not sharing with Mrs. Lee at the moment.

He heard enough of the conversation to know the two were intimate. Now he knew what this meant, for he was truly one of them—he was a Christian! And Christians seem to have special ways of communicating.

The silence was broken with an abrupt statement from Mrs. Lee. "I have notified Mr. Lee. He should be home as quickly as he can get transportation. I hope he doesn't worry too much and get himself hurt attempting to get here quickly." Mrs. Lee's words were somewhat rambling. She was greatly disturbed. Yong-soo was her only child; her fears and apprehensions knew no limits. The only thing that kept her within the bounds of sanity was the calmness of Mr. Kim and Pastor Choi.

The next to arrive at the hospital was Chang, Hee-sung. He burst through the door, telling that everyone in Imja Dong had heard about the accident. It seemed the local police took the taxi driver to the Dong station, and all of the Dong officials had learned about it.

Hee-sung heard of the incident through a young traffic policeman who had been his classmate in high school.

Soon-sik gave Hee-sung all the information available. Then, as the two talked, Soon confided in Hee-sung as to why he and Yong had been walking down by the river.

"Hee-sung, I know you led Yong to the Lord, and you need to know that today I asked Jesus to come into my life. He has been so real to me in these last few minutes."

There are times when smiles break the tension of disasters. This was one of those times. Hee-sung's young and vigorous face flashed a smile.

"Oh, praise God, Soon-sik. Thank you for sharing this with me.

I shall pray for you and help you in any way the Lord leads!" In the midst of a terrible time, these two shared the assurance of the presence of God.

As the word spread in Imja Dong, the genuine concern for Yong, mixed with curiosity as to the accident, led many to rush to the hospital. The waiting room became crowded and noisy. The same questions, How did it happen? Is he alive? How badly is he injured? were asked repeatedly.

Suddenly the room became quiet. Two uniformed policemen with a rather pale and timid-looking man by their side walked into the waiting room, causing all eyes to turn to the reception desk.

"Please, I'm Policeman Park, and this is Policeman Koh. This is taxi driver Suh, Tae-woo. We have come to inquire about the condition of one Lee, Yong-soo. Can you help us?"

The receptionist reached for her telephone and spoke briefly into it. Replacing the telephone, she said, "The doctor will be right out." Before she could finish, all eyes turned to the emergency room door to see the doctor emerge.

"Is this the driver of the taxi?" Dr. Chang asked, not waiting for an introduction to the policemen, yet addressing his remarks to them.

"Yes, but how is the young man? Is he alive?" Policeman Park inquired.

"Yes, we have him in radiology right now. He's broken up, and we need to determine the extent of his injuries. If he's not bleeding internally, we should be able to save him. His vital signs improved considerably, so I could send him up to radiology."

The doctor continued, "I'm concerned too about his head injuries. It looked as though he may have a fracture or a severe concussion. Whatever, we'll know in a few moments."

As the doctor spoke, the elevator opened; a nurse emerged. She saw the doctor and stopped, waiting for him to come to her. It was to be a private conversation.

Turning to the large group in the room, Dr. Chang asked, "Are Yong's parents here?" With this he moved to a quiet corner. Mrs. Lee stepped out, saying, "I'm Yong's mother."

Mr. Kim stepped over to stand by Mrs. Lee's side. The doctor spoke in a quiet voice. He greeted the two as Mrs. Lee introduced her friend Mr. Kim. She half mumbled something about Mr. Lee trying to get here from work. "I'm sure he's on his way. He works in another city." The doctor nodded.

"Mrs. Lee, your son has a fractured skull. It is along the bottom part, the base of his skull. I don't know the extent of this injury. The radiologist tells us that there is a broken shoulder, his left; there are five broken ribs. He does not see any internal injuries, but we'll continue to monitor this carefully in the next few hours.

"There's nothing we can do for the fractured skull. The bleeding on the inside is critical. Too much bleeding, and the pressure will kill him. If he needs surgery, it will be determined by the neurologist. We can take a scan of his brain and see about the pressure. With such injuries we have to wait and see. We'll take the scan now and let the neurologist decide about surgery and treatment."

With that Dr. Chang paused for a moment as if waiting for questions. Mrs. Lee did not respond; she seemed to be in shock. Mr. Kim was attending to his friends's needs and felt he should not ask questions. Both had heard of such injuries. If Yong survived, they knew it would be a long fight.

Pastor Choi organized those in the waiting room into a silent group sharing a quiet vigil.

Yong's Bible and Sunday School teachers came to the hospital, along with the leaders of Imja Dong Church. This gave Pastor Choi an opportunity he had known before in similar situations. He asked them to form a circle, join hands, and have silent prayer for Yong.

Mrs. Lee noticed the men and women forming circles. She did not know what they were doing, but felt she was somewhat familiar with their posture. They were praying.

The two policemen were still there with the taxi driver. Mrs. Lee moved to the reception desk and spoke to the taxi driver.

"I'm Mrs. Lee. Can you tell me what happened?" It was her first opportunity to address the driver directly, and she needed to know about the accident.

"Mrs. Lee, it had just gotten dark. Shortly after turning my headlights on, I came to the bend in the river road. I was blinded by the lights of the oncoming cars. I never saw your son until he was in the air. I'm so sorry. Oh, I don't know what I'll do now. Driving is my life, and it seems as though they are going to take my license. This is my first serious accident. Please tell these people and your husband how sorry I am and that I did not see your son walking in the road."

It was the plea of a broken man. His heart and Mrs. Lee's had something of the same feeling at that moment. One because he had hit the young man, and the other because the young man was her only son.

The policemen stepped forward to give their regrets to Mrs. Lee;

and to affirm the driver's statement about the inability to see on the road and the fact that oncoming lights did blind drivers in the bend of the road. They spoke about Yong not being able to see the taxi and Soon not having time to warn his friend. With that they excused themselves and started for the door with the driver.

As they reached the door, the driver turned to speak to Mrs. Lee as an afterthought, but so all could hear. "Mrs. Lee, don't worry about the hospital costs. My company will take care of anything your son needs!"

At that moment, in time to hear the remarks, Mr. Lee appeared from a side door. He had come from the front of the hospital down to the waiting room. Mrs. Lee saw her husband and rushed to fall into his arms. Now her tears began to flow, and the reassuring pats on the back did not stem the tide.

"Oh, I'm so glad you're here; our son is in bad condition!" she sobbed. Lee, Soon-suk could barely understand his wife. He stepped back from her, and turning to Mr. Kim, said, "What happened, sir?"

Mr. Kim told about the two young men going to the river for a quiet talk. Then he told of the accident, the doctor's preliminary report, and something of the tentative prognosis.

With that Mr. Lee dropped his head for a moment. When he lifted his head, he noticed for the first time the huge gathering of people. He looked at them quizzically.

His questions were answered as his eyes caught the group holding hands with heads bowed. They had been in the position for a long time. He asked Mr. Kim if these were people he knew.

With that question, Pastor Choi stepped forward. Placing his arm around Mr. Lee, he said, "Sir, your son has many Christian friends. You met a few of them at his baptism. Now the entire church has been mobilized to pray for Yong. These are but a few of those who are praying right now!"

Lee, Soon-suk was moved in his heart in that moment more than at any time he could remember. He instinctively reached out for his wife and drew her to him.

Mr. Kim stepped to their side. He spoke quietly. "Today your son walked with Cho, Soon-sik to the river. It seems Soon wanted to know how to become a Christian. Yong was his lifelong and best friend. He knew Yong would tell him the way."

It was a quiet, almost sacred, tone Mr. Kim used as he continued. "After Yong shared with Soon, they started home. They never made it. While Soon waited here alone, he asked the Lord to come into his life. He became a Christian. For this you should be proud."

Mr. Kim's final remark was one the Lees would remember for years to come. "Dear friends, we have a word from God about disaster for Christians. It simply says that 'all things work together for good to them that love God, to them who are the called according to his purpose.'"

Mr. Kim concluded, "We have seen how God has used this time to bless Soon-sik. It will be interesting to see what happens when all things work together for good, under His hand."

Yong's parents gazed into each other's eyes. Neither seemed to know what all of this meant.

They became aware of the quiet waiting room. Turning slowly, they noticed the small groups of people holding hands, with heads bowed. Mr. Kim heard Mrs. Lee say as she leaned her head on her husband's chest, "Maybe someday we'll understand it. Right now it seems like a nightmare."

CHAPTER 14

Amazing Grace

It was one of the longest nights the Lees had ever known. Yong was removed from radiology to the intensive care ward. A nurse came down about 11:00 to say they were moving the young patient.

Mr. Lee asked if he could see his son. The nurse told him it would be permissible in a short while. There was some work which needed to be done before anyone could see the patient.

Many of those who came to the hospital in the early evening gave their words of concern and sympathy to the parents and excused themselves.

Pastor Choi stayed, encouraging the family from time to time. He gave pastoral instructions to those of his congregation who had spent much time in individual and group prayer.

The Lees wanted to speak to Soon-sik. They asked if he could stay a little longer. He said he thought he wanted to stay all night. Mr. Kim spoke to the group, telling them what the nurse had told the Lees concerning Yong. He told them he was taking the Lees up to the third floor of the hospital to the intensive care ward waiting area. He spoke to the group, "Anyone who wants to go can come along."

As they started to leave, Mr. Lee stepped to the reception desk to speak to the young woman on duty. "Young lady, please tell those in the emergency room, and especially Dr. Chang, how much we appreciate their kindness to our son and our friends. We have been here several hours now; you've been most kind. We'll remember your thoughtfulness to us."

This brought a strong smile and a bow from the young woman. Seldom did she get those remarks from people she served, as the situation was always tense and hurried in her area.

The group moved onto the elevator. When they stepped off on the third floor, a nurse was waiting to take it. "Please, can you tell us something about our son, Lee, Yong-soo? He was brought up here a few minutes ago." As Mr. Lee spoke these words, he was looking over the nurse's shoulder to see if anyone was going or coming from the intensive care ward. As he saw no one, his attention turned to the nurse.

"No, sir, Mr. Lee. There is no word yet. Dr. Yoo, Sung-nam is our staff neurosurgeon. He heads the neurosurgery department here in our school of medicine. He and his assistants have been examining your son for some time now, reading the X-rays and checking his vital signs. He should be out shortly to tell you his preliminary diagnosis."

With this, the young nurse disappeared into the elevator, and the group settled down to wait for some word from the ward.

It was nearly 12:30 when Mr. Lee remembered he needed to talk to Soon-sik. Yong's friend sat quietly beside Mr. Kim. The two were almost asleep; it had been a long and tiring day.

Soon was somewhat startled by Mr. Lee's nudge as he sat down beside the tired and worried young man.

"Tell me, Soon, was Yong in good spirits today?" Mr. Lee began. He thought a casual remark would be the best and most gentle way to open the conversation.

"Yes, sir, he was, and we had a great day. It was our first opportunity in weeks to get away from our studies and home chores, so we could be alone for a talk. You know, we once played together each afternoon. Then we could talk on our way home. But Yong and I have been busy this school year. I needed to have this special talk with him.

"We decided to go to our favorite place down by the river. Some months ago Yong got me started in his Bible class on Fridays. I've been studying the Bible regularly now. There were some things I felt Yong could explain to me. Mr. Lee, we had the best talk; time slipped by so quickly. It was dark before we realized it was getting late."

This was something of an explanation, but it sounded much like an apology. "Son," Yong's father stopped Soon-sik with that word, indicating his desire to speak. "Mrs. Lee and I are most happy you and Yong have been friends most of your lives. We hear your name every day at the house. Yong loves you dearly. You must not apologize for two friends wanting to talk. I know that desire. I have a close friend too.

"Now," Mr. Lee continued, "we want you to know we've talked to the officer who investigated the accident. He assures me you did not have time to warn Yong before he was hit. We want you to go on home now and come back tomorrow after school. If there's any change in Yong's condition, we'll call you first."

Mr. Kim heard all the conversation. He was like a member of the family now to Mr. Lee. After all he had done for Yong, with the help he had given in times of crisis, Mr. Kim had been closer to the Lees than many members of their own family.

When Mr. Lee finished talking to Soon, Mr. Kim endorsed the instructions for him to go on home and get some rest. He added his words of assurance about notification if anything developed.

Pastor Choi remained. He alternately prayed and napped as the group dwindled. He was awakened somewhat when members of the Lee family began to gather. They had to come into Imja Dong from distant areas and had been traveling since early evening. Each new arrival wanted to be briefed on the events of the day and Yong's present condition. The Lees and Mr. Kim took turns with this task.

Mr. Lee's family had not been able to be close, since he worked out of the city and was away from home when one of the members made an unscheduled trip to see Mrs. Lee and Yong in Imja Dong. They were able to gather only at Chusok, the Korean traditional family observance of thanksgiving in the fall, and once or twice during the balance of the year. Like all good Korean families, they gathered quickly, however, when there was difficulty. This was such a time.

Mr. Lee had two sisters living; a brother had died when they were young and both parents later. The sisters were Christians. When they were introduced to Pastor Choi, they rejoiced with him that Yong had made a profession of faith in the Lord Jesus Christ. Then they asked for the pastor to lead the three of them in a prayer of thanks for a safe journey for them and to intercede once again with them for Yong.

As the three gathered to pray, Soon left for his home. The other members of the group, some friends, and other family settled down for the wait. All were thinking of the report the doctor was to bring, for they had been told of his anticipated diagnosis.

It was nearly 2:00 in the morning when Dr. Yoo came to the waiting area asking for Mr. Lee. Of the nearly 20 people who were waiting, almost all came quickly to their feet.

Mr. and Mrs. Lee identified themselves to the doctor. "I'm Dr. Yoo, staff neurosurgeon. Since Dr. Chang admitted your son early last evening, we have been doing studies and keeping close watch on his vital signs. He is stable right now, but we have him on the critical list."

The doctor spoke so most of those waiting could hear him. After the opening remark, he lowered his voice, speaking now to the Lees, Mr. Kim, and Pastor Choi. Family and friends gathered in the tight circle, attempting to hear the conversation.

"We have a difficult job if Lee, Yong-soo is to survive." The doctor addressed the Lees. "Dr. Chang's preliminary diagnosis was correct. Yong has a severe fracture at the base of his skull. There is some swelling outside, as if he hit his head on the curb. We don't know how much swelling is on the inside. It is *that* pressure which is critical. But your son is strong and in good health. The internal specialists have looked at him and they don't believe he is injured there except for his broken ribs. They didn't puncture his lungs or any other vital organs. His broken shoulder should heal without difficulty."

The doctor's report was concise and to the point. It did not build hope, but neither did it cause panic.

As Dr. Yoo turned to leave, he gave his instructions. This time he spoke to the group. "We have several very ill patients in the ward. We will allow one of you to be with Yong, unless we ask you to leave. You can assist the nurses if they ask, but otherwise please do not attempt to wait on the patient. In his condition we must be very careful with him. I'll check Yong four or five times a day and when called as long as he is critical. If you need to ask questions, address them to the duty nurses. They will get in touch with me if there is something we need to talk over."

All who heard the doctor began mumbling their thanks. The family, having no questions, reached out to each other while Mr. Lee shook the doctor's hand. Pastor Choi moved to him quickly and assured him many were praying for Yong and those who were on the healing team. The doctor disappeared into the intensive care ward.

Mr. Lee, speaking quietly to his wife, said, "I want you to go in and stay with Yong. I'll go in for a brief visit, and then you stay for the night. My sisters and I will relieve you and stay with him tomorrow."

Without a word, Mrs. Lee moved quietly into the intensive care ward. It was a strange place to her, and she was very careful not to disturb any of the patients, as the doctor had instructed. For the first time in her life she saw the hurt and trauma of humanity gathered there in metal beds and plain white sheets. She was to become very familiar with the austerity and sterility of the place in the days ahead.

When dawn appeared in the window of the waiting area, it greeted a scattered and tired group. As they stirred, some went for coffee. Others sought a place to wash their faces, attend to personal grooming, and other matters.

Mr. Kim suggested a plan for the day. He and Pastor Choi would stay in the waiting area to brief guests on Yong's condition; Mrs. Lee would go home, change clothes, rest, and eat. She would come again in the afternoon; then Mr. Lee could go and do the same. The sisters would join their brother, each having some time in the ward, and all going to the Lee home together later. Some of the leading members of the church would come to keep vigil in the waiting area at all times.

To all of this there was general agreement. As soon as Mrs. Lee came from the ward, one of the sisters would go in for a couple of hours, and the schedule would be in effect.

For breakfast Mr. Lee had coffee and a piece of cake purchased at the hospital snack shop. Through the night he had been joining others at the coffee machine. Now eating meant nothing to him; his mind was with Yong.

As he was settling down to wait his turn in the ward, he noticed a well-dressed gentleman emerge from the elevator. He stood up to greet the guest.

"Mr. Lee, I'm Choi, Tae-won, chairman of the Hankook Furniture Company. Last night I brought your son to the emergency room with another young man. I haven't slept too well and I couldn't get any information from the nurses on the telephone, so I felt I had to come by and see about your son."

"Thank you, thank you, Mr. Choi. My son's young friend, Soon-sik, told us about you, but said he didn't get your name or have a moment to give you a word of appreciation. Our son is stable but critical. He's got a fractured skull. It will take some time before we know his true condition. We appreciate your assistance in bringing our son to the hospital. You may have saved his life."

As Mr. Lee spoke, the gentleman raised his hand as if to stop the remarks. He was expressing humility.

Then he added, "This morning, I called the president of Hanyang Taxi Company; he's an old classmate of mine. It was his taxi driver that hit your son. He said to tell you he would see you today. He said your son will have every care and consideration humanly possible. They kept his driver overnight at the police station. The man is in terrible shape, I understand."

"We're very sorry for him," and as he spoke, Mr. Lee dropped his head. "It's not a good situation for any of us. I don't wish the driver any harm. Maybe they will let him return to his home today. Help him, sir, if you can."

The last remark touched the heart of the new friend. He excused himself. No sooner had he disappeared than the Mr. Choi whose name had been mentioned appeared. He was followed by officials of the railway system for whom Mr. Lee worked.

So it went most of the morning. The entire community was expressing sincere concern for Lee, Yong-soo, and the Lees were deeply moved.

It was routine after the first three days—no change in the patient and a long vigil at the bedside. Mr. Kim took the place of Mrs. Lee some evenings. He would read his Bible and pray and quite frequently speak quietly to Yong about the Lord and other godly concerns, as if Yong could hear him.

Mr. Lee's sisters returned home a short time after the accident. The days were long for Yong's father. He spent more time with his son in those six weeks than at any other time of their lives. He wished it had been under different circumstances.

Late one afternoon, just before Mrs. Lee was coming to take up the bedside watch, Dr. Yoo appeared at Yong's bed.

"Mr. Lee, as your son is still in this coma, we have to make a decision which is important. The internal swelling seems to have subsided. There is no reason for his continuance in a comatose condition unless there is something we've missed and we can't see in the scan. As you know, we've scanned his brain every four or five days since he arrived. I'm going to make a suggestion."

"Yes, sir, Dr. Yoo. What do you suggest?" There was some anxiety in Mr. Lee's voice. This was the first decision he had been called on to make since the accident occurred.

"I believe there may be a small embolism, a blood clot, at the point of the fracture. If that is the case, we either have to remove or dissolve it. Both procedures have some danger. If you give me your permission, I'll put some dye in the artery, it's an arteriogram, and we'll see if something is blocking the blood circulation. I don't make any promises, but we'll be better informed about Yong's condition."

"Dr. Yoo, Mrs. Lee should return from home in a few minutes. I'll talk to her and we'll sign the consent papers as soon as possible.

You know we really appreciate all you and your staff have done for us; we'll never forget it."

Shortly after the conversation ended, Mrs. Lee slipped into the ward. Making her way to Yong's bed, she could see anxiety in her husband's face. "Is something wrong? What's happened?" He explained the procedure which Dr. Yoo had suggested.

When Mr. Lee completed his report, Mrs. Lee sighed and whispered, "Thank goodness. I knew something needed to be done. Let him get on with it."

The nurse told Mrs. Lee the doctor had given orders to reduce Yong's fever, which had persisted since the accident. He had an elevation of two or three degrees temperature above normal. The doctor wanted it near normal for the procedure.

Mrs. Lee helped the nurses reduce the fever. They bathed him in alcohol and applied ice packs to his body. Yong never moved. If he knew anything was happening, there was no outward sign. It was as if he were dead.

The procedure was performed. When Yong was brought back to the ward, there were many nurses, but Dr. Yoo was not with them. The family and friends waited anxiously for the report.

When Dr. Yoo stepped from the elevator, there was a smile on his face. "I knew it. It just had to be there. There was a small embolism in the artery at the base of the skull. I don't know, but I think it may have moved when we traced the artery. We'll wait a couple of days and see what happens. I'm encouraged for the first time, and I hope the Lees are too." With those words, the doctor went quickly into the ward.

It was guarded enthusiasm, but it was, nevertheless, the first reason for anyone to smile since that fateful night nearly seven weeks ago. As Pastor Choi had said many times, "God has heard the prayers of those who have been praying around the clock for these weeks. I know it." The Lees were hoping beyond all hope that the pastor was right.

Mr. Lee stepped to the telephone to call Mr. Kim with the news. He said he would be right over after closing his store.

As soon as he received the call, he phoned Pastor Choi. The pastor notified the group which had been praying at the church. It was now time for renewed effort for those who wanted God to perform a miracle for their young friend.

Though it was time for Mrs. Lee to be with Yong, Mr. Kim asked if he could spend some time with him. Mrs. Lee agreed. Mr. Kim eased into the ward, noticing the new arrangement of intravenous containers and the oxygen equipment. It had been changed while Yong was in the operating room.

For some time Mr. Kim read his Bible, talked with God, and looked intently at Yong. For some unknown reason, he began to hum very quietly. Then he began to sing softly, "Amazing grace! How sweet the sound, That saved a wretch like me! I once was lost, but now am found, Was blind, but now I see."

He paused in his singing, for something strange was happening. The bed moved slightly. Then he saw it. Yong opened his eyes!

A muffled sound came through the oxygen mask. It was weak and barely audible. "Amazing grace! How sweet the sound." The words trailed off, the eyes closed slowly, then came open even wider.

"Mr. Kim, you've been singing our song."

With these words, the tears began to course down the old shopkeeper's cheeks. The nurses heard him give a brief sob, and thinking the worst, rushed to the bed.

"Oh, he's awake. Call Dr. Yoo. He's awake!"

The rushing around had given Mr. Kim time to slip out into the waiting area, a place which now seemed like a second home to the many who had spent time there in the weeks of waiting. None noticed Mr. Kim except Yong's mother. With one glance into his face, she almost shouted, "What's the matter? I better go!"

As she started to the door, Mr. Kim took her arm. "Wait, Mrs. Lee. Yong's awake—he's come back from the dead. They've called Dr. Yoo."

Mrs. Lee rushed through the door. She was just two steps ahead of the doctor who had come up from making afternoon rounds. He spoke as he took quick steps toward Yong's bed.

"Well, I'm amazed, Mrs. Lee, I'm amazed. Seems like God has worked a miracle. They tell me our patient is back with the living."

In the next few minutes, all of the anxiety and pain of the last weeks was forgotten. Friends began to gather. Tales were told of the hours of prayer and the hopes of schoolmates as well as the entire community.

Mr. Kim told Pastor Choi about the song and how Yong had sung it after him. The pastor couldn't wait to tell the Lees about how Mr. Kim and Yong had shared their most intimate song in the moment their son regained consciousness.

Before the pastor could share this with the Lees, they asked for an audience with him. They wanted to express their gratitude for all the church had been doing, and asked the pastor to tell them on Sunday.

"Too," Mr. Lee added, "since we attended that baptismal service of Yong's, we've discussed the matter of our own needs. It seems these last few weeks have pointed out to us we need to be Christians, Pastor, and we want to have an opportunity to talk to you about it soon."

As Pastor Choi stepped over to tell Mr. Kim that bit of news, he heard the dear old man in beautiful tones singing, "Amazing grace! How sweet the sound."

Yes, thought the pastor, God's grace is amazing, and we have experienced it here today!

CHAPTER 15

Hill Difficulty

Six more weeks passed before Lee, Yong-soo could remember any of the details of the night of the accident. The one thing which kept coming to his mind in those days was the battle of Christian, after he had been to the cross, in John Bunyan's story.

It seemed Yong made some remark to Mr. Kim about the ordeal of one who had been converted. He remembered Mr. Kim said, "The way of the Christian is not free from difficulty."

The Korean saying, The bird with the broken wing gets the attention of the mother bird, was true in Yong's case. His mother centered her attention on her son and made every provision for his recovery in the long days in the hospital.

She made arrangements for Cho, Soon-sik to keep a record of all of the assignments in his school work. She saw to it her son did not lose a valuable year in his education.

In the tenth week of recuperation, Yong began to catch up on his studies. His older friend Chang, Hee-sung started to college, and Mrs. Lee appealed to him to visit Yong to help with his studies.

Soon and Hee were devoted to their Christian brother and took great pride in helping Yong. Mrs. Lee suggested to the principal of his school that her son could take his exams when his class was ready for them if they were made available to him.

Dr. Yoo, Sung-nam continued to tell everyone Yong was his miracle patient. He was elated to see him able to do his studies.

There were several events which marked the four months of Yong's recuperation at the hospital. His time was spent in studying, exercising, and having sessions in therapy. Yet Yong had some time to spend with Mr. Kim. They had long discussions in the afternoon when his Christian friend could get someone to keep the store.

One matter that Yong wanted Mr. Kim to clarify had to do with the taxi driver who hit him. When questioned, Mr. Kim said, "Yong, that man had a difficult time. He was away from work for several weeks. The court charged him a stiff fine, but told him to return to work.

"When I heard he had not returned to work, I asked Pastor Choi to go with me to visit him. He lives on the north side of Seoul and attends a small Christian church. Pastor Choi contacted his pastor, and the three of us had a nice visit with him. We had prayer with him.

"Yong, the driver's pastor indicated that the man had been lax on church attendance, working most Sundays. I received word recently that he had returned to church, renewed his vows to the Lord, and was receiving personal attention from his pastor for Christian growth. He has since returned to work, but he is not driving on Sundays."

This news touched Yong's heart. "Just another good thing that comes from something bad, eh, Mr. Kim?" A smile coursed Mr. Kim's face, an indication of total agreement.

This good news and warm response was a reminder to Yong that there was another beautiful experience that he needed to share with Mr. Kim. "Sir," Yong began slowly, as he was not sure how his friend would receive what he was about to reveal. "Sir, I had something else to tell you." Before he could finish, Mr. Kim interrupted. "Well, what is it, son? We have no secrets, and there is nothing we can't share."

With this encouragement, Yong began to tell how he had a vision when he was in the intensive care ward. He told Mr. Kim he saw two figures clothed in white robes with a brilliant radiance about them.

In his vision he saw the beautiful figure of one very large smiling individual reaching his hand out to the two figures clothed in white.

As he recalled the vision to Mr. Kim, he said, "I saw the two figures coming closer to the other one. I noticed there were great black spots on the white robes. Then they fell down at the feet of the other figure. When he reached down to touch them, I saw the nail prints! It was Jesus!

"As He touched them, the spots disappeared; there was now a brilliance about the three of them I had never seen before."

Continuing, Yong said, "Mr. Kim, a hand reached down with a book opened to a blank page. Another hand was extended with a writing pen. The two figures were kneeling, weeping; their bodies shaking.

"Jesus took the pen and wrote something in the book. As He

turned to close the book, I heard Him say, 'This is the Lamb's Book of Life'! I saw the names He had written. Mr. Kim, they were Lee, Soon-suk and Oh, Soo-won, my father and mother!"

Once again, these two were sharing sacred secrets. It seemed this was their destiny.

When Yong finished relating his vision to Mr. Kim, he noticed his dear old friend's eyes filled with tears. It was a glorious time of sharing, but they had not finished.

"Yong, we have not told you because Dr. Yoo didn't want to get you too excited. Several weeks after your accident, your father and mother went to see Pastor Choi. They told him of their feelings and their private discussions as to what they experienced at your baptism. Too, they were distraught they could not join the multitude of Christian friends who were praying for your recovery. You know your friends met at church around the clock praying for you these six weeks."

Yong listened, and before Mr. Kim could answer, asked, "But what did that have to do with my parents?"

"Son, three days before you came back to the land of the living, your father and mother accepted Jesus Christ as their Saviour. When I told them you had opened your eyes while I was singing "Amazing Grace," both of them said it was because God heard their prayers for the first time.

"Both indicated they'd tried to pray and received no satisfaction. They said it was more like wishing than praying. When they came to Christ, they felt the way was opened for true prayer."

As Mr. Kim spoke, Yong glanced over his friend's shoulder to see his mother come into the room. Reaching out his hand, he burst into tears, frightening Mrs. Lee.

"Son, what's the matter? Have you had pain today? How is your head?" Yong could not answer; just shook his head from side to side as a negative answer to the questions.

"Then tell me, son, what is it?"

Mr. Kim reached up to take Mrs. Lee's arm and gently restrained her. "Mrs. Lee, I just shared with Yong-soo that you and Mr. Lee had asked Jesus Christ to come into your lives. He is overwhelmed with joy, and we must be careful he doesn't get too excited."

Without a word, mother fell on her son's shoulder with a tender embrace, respecting his injured shoulder now almost healed. It was a deep and meaningful moment. They sobbed softly.

Mr. Kim slipped out of the room and stopped a nurse about to enter with, "Please, dear, Mrs. Lee and her son need a few moments alone. There is no cause for alarm, they are just sharing something personal."

The knowledge that he would get to see his parents baptized made the days of study and weary waiting pass somewhat faster.

Yong's father had said on his last visit they were praying for Yong to be prepared to take his college entrance examination. It was the first time he heard his father mention prayer. Since he spoke of it in regard to Yong's future, it made the son humbly proud. His own prayertime each evening got longer and more filled with praise since his parents became Christians.

Mr. Kim shared with Yong on one occasion that his savings account, which was started several summers ago, had increased quite a bit with contributions from the taxi company and friends of the family.

Mr. Kim knew Mr. Lee would never tell his son these personal matters. When he shared it, he said, "Your father is very proud of you, Yong. He wants you to get a good education. Every dollar of the money will be used for your education. Your account here at the hospital has been paid, coming from several sources. You have a great future ahead of you. Just study hard."

In *The Pilgrim's Progress,* Yong remembered Christian got great satisfaction out of each obstacle he overcame. He was reminded that Christian learned new lessons from the Lord with each difficulty.

Yong reflected on the course of his own journey since Christ called him into His kingdom. While thinking on these things one afternoon, he noticed a young man in a wheelchair being rolled onto the hospital sun porch. The spring season had brought with it a warming sunshine. The long winter was over, and it seemed the two young men had decided they wanted to have some time out of their rooms.

Yong was about to be released from the hospital. He had passed his school exams, and his father was ecstatic over his high marks.

When Chang, Hee-sung had come from his college on the weekend, he brought the good news that Yong had passed among the top scorers on the entrance exam. This meant he should get the school of his choice! It was a victory over pain, boredom, and confinement.

Yong was reflecting on all the developments of the last three and one-half months. He did not expect to meet anyone he knew. He wanted a few minutes in the sunshine to praise God and meditate.

"How are you?" came a female voice, from one whom Yong-soo had not noticed. She had pushed the other patient's wheelchair onto the porch.

"It looks like you wanted to get some sun too. My brother has been asking me all afternoon to bring him to the sun porch. He's getting well enough to complain, and I think it's time for him to go home."

Yong was overwhelmed. The voice's owner was an attractive young woman who seemed to be about his age. He was anxious to answer her, to keep the conversation going.

"Well, I've been so busy studying and taking exams. My father arranged for the teachers to come to the hospital for my high school exams. They took me in an ambulance to the university for the college entrance exams.

"My father has been very good to me since I have been here. I wanted to please him, and I haven't had time for anything except therapy and study. Two of my friends have been coming to help me with my studies."

Now Yong was rambling, telling personal things no one had heard from him before. It was doubtful if the two new friends cared to hear all of this, but he wanted them to know he was interested in talking to them.

When he finished, the young woman said, "My name is Yoo, In-ja. What's yours?"

"Mine?" Yong blurted. "It's Lee, Yong-soo."

"Well, Mr. Lee, don't expect too much conversation from my brother. His name is Yoo, Yong-won. He fell at school and hit his face on a piece of concrete. His jaw is broken, and they have it wired. He can speak, but it's very awkward and slow. He makes sign language to me. We have pretty good understanding, but he gets me confused. Then he gets angry if I don't know what he's trying to tell me."

"I'm sorry about your accident, Yoo, Yong-won."

As he spoke, Yong leaned over to look closer at his new acquaintance's jaw.

"It looks like it's healing good; how many stitches did they take in the cut?"

"I believe it was 45 or 50. He was in the operating room a long time while they set his jaw and sewed up the cut. I thought they'd never get through. My mother was frightened to death because she saw Yong-won bleeding so badly. She thought he was going to die!"

As Yoo, In-ja spoke, Yong felt it was awful he would meet such an attractive young woman in, of all places, the hospital, where he couldn't even walk her home!

That first visit lasted more than an hour. Yoo, In-ja shared her desires to enter college and told something of her success as a student. She had been chosen to represent the school in two senior projects and was given the outstanding scholarship award. Yong thought that beauty had been joined with brains; it was a delightful combination as far as he was concerned.

In the days following, the two met several times on the sun porch and in the hospital corridor. In-ja's brother had the wires removed from his jaw and was able to join the conversation. He wanted to talk about the soccer team of which he was a member; Yong wanted to talk about In-ja; and In-ja talked about anything that came to her mind. The three had many afternoons together, as study time was not a priority now.

Lee, Yong-soo was to be released after Dr. Yoo gave him a thorough examination. He hoped he would see In-ja one more time, so they could plan a meeting for the future.

It didn't happen. When Yong-soo was taken to the waiting taxi, he had mixed emotions. He was happy to be leaving what he had come to call home. He came to the hospital like a dead person; he was now leaving under his own power. The blackness that had covered his mind was gone. He was praising God!

The blackness was replaced with beautiful memories of prayers, visits, kindness, concern, and, most of all, the knowledge that God used this event to bring his parents to a saving knowledge of the Lord.

He remembered the pleasant visits of Yoo, In-ja, the bright and talented young woman of the sun porch. He wondered if he would ever see her again. This gave him feelings he could not identify, for he had never felt such attraction to a girl.

As he started for home, Yong had serious thoughts. He told his mother, "It has been long and arduous. It brought anxiety and pain to me, but each experience has brought beautiful victories. I am blessed of God!"

With those thoughts, he heard his mother say to the taxi driver, "Sir, please take us to Imja Dong." By God's grace, he was headed home. He had climbed Hill Difficulty.

CHAPTER 16

The Youngest Pilgrim

The most difficult thing Yong faced after the gladness of the homecoming had worn off was fatigue. His accident, recuperation, and the long period of studying left him without strength.

It became the work of Yong's mother to restore her son to his former vigor. At one time she had worried about his long hours of school and his Bible studies. Now she would be delighted for him to be able to get back to his routine.

Day after day friends of Yong's mother came by to see how they could help. Some would bring dishes of food; others would stay to do the laundry or make a trip to the market for the Lee family. Imja Dong was a good community, and the people were close.

Since Mrs. Lee had become a Christian, her circle of friends had increased. She wanted to grow in Christ; therefore, she invited some of the women to come by and spend time with her in personal Bible studies when Yong was resting.

For three months, mother and son spent most of the hours of the day with one another. They frequently discussed Bible verses. Yong was able to give his mother insight into many of the truths he learned since becoming a Christian.

When Yong's father came for the weekend, they talked about the church. One of the parents attended worship each Lord's Day. They became very close, and all three were praying for Yong's full recovery, so he could attend his college classes.

His close friend Cho, Soon-sik stopped to visit frequently. He told Yong of some discussion in the Bible class and the latest news at the church.

They discussed the prospects for the new school year and how they would be following in the steps of their older friend Chang, Hee-sung at college. Both had been successful in getting their first choice of schools; they had chosen the same one.

God was blessing. Hee-sung talked with Soon-sik about joining the Christian club at school. He said the group was looking forward to having both of the new students in school with them for the next term.

Yong's days of praying for physical and spiritual strength, with his exercises, began to pay big dividends. When he visited the doctor for a checkup, he was told that he could begin taking short walks and visiting in the neighborhood. In fact, Dr. Yoo encouraged Yong-soo to start some light outdoor exercise, suggesting a little athletics would be permitted if done in moderation.

Mr. Kim watched the calendar for the day Yong could get permission to come for a visit. That was the first place Yong wanted to go as soon as the doctor gave the word. With Dr. Yoo's release Yong headed for the corner store.

"My, you're a wonderful sight, young man; just like you'd never been in an accident. We've missed you around here. Our customers ask about you every day. Son, you've got a lot of friends. They all tell me they've been praying for you."

Mr. Kim's greeting overwhelmed Yong. "Sir, there's never been a day I haven't thought about you, and I've thanked God for your friendship. I know I'm the most blessed young man in all of Imja Dong."

Yong had waited many months to be able to tell Mr. Kim how much he loved him. Too, he wanted to tell him how God had used his old friend to bless the Lee family.

"Yong, did you know when you became a Christian that your parents and Soon-sik would follow in your steps? There's no telling what God will do when someone yields to the convicting power of His Spirit. Old Satan has been trying to get you off track with that accident, with all you've been through. You've been faithful, and God has honored your faithfulness."

Once again, the wisdom and steady influence of Mr. Kim was blessing the heart and mind of Lee, Yong-soo.

It was a glad reunion, shortened only by the appearance of Mrs. Lee. Giving her bows of appreciation, and showing her gratitude to Mr. Kim with a beautiful smile, she said, "I thought I'd find you here. I saw Dr. Yoo's nurse and she told me of the release he gave Yong and the good news. So, I thought maybe I should come by and lead you home. I don't want you to do too much and get tired. You two never know when to stop when you're visiting."

When the first day of school finally came, Yong and Soon were the first to check their classes. After filling out forms and receiving their assignments, they discussed mutual needs.

The first thing they needed to know was the layout of the campus. It was a large place; all of the buildings looked the same.

It was good to have an upperclassman like Chang, Hee-sung. As they were about to explore the grounds to find their way through the big buildings, Hee showed up with three friends.

"Hey, you guys, we've been looking for you. I know you want to find your way around the campus, and we're here to show you." The two new students were glad to see Hee-sung, who had been a real blessing to Yong. Now it seemed that God was using him again in a time of need.

Yong reported all of the events of the day to Mr. Kim. He gave words of advice. "Study hard, son, and make good marks. You are a walking miracle. God will use you to help others someday if you continue to be faithful with your time and abilities."

It was always like this with Mr. Kim: a word of encouragement or some word of direction as to how to be an instrument of God.

The first year of Yong's school went with great speed. Because of his lack of strength, there was not too much that he could do except study.

One of his professors, Dr. Song, Dong-won, stopped Yong after class one day to tell him the news of the accident. He said the miracle of his recovery had been discussed by a number of students in their discussions after classes. He encouraged Yong to study hard and take advantage of the fact he was really having a second chance at life.

Because of the need to study, and because he was still lacking in stamina, Yong did not join the Christian club. Cho, Soon-sik accepted Hee's invitation. He kept Yong informed of club activities. Yong had to receive his information about school life from others; he spent most of his time in the library.

There were those times when studying took all of his energy and strength. For rejuvenation he would place his head on the library table to rest for brief periods, frequently taking short naps.

It was at such a time when he was almost into a good sleep, he heard, "Are you still recuperating?" Yong jerked his head up. He knew the voice. It was Yoo, In-ja!

"What are you doing in this library?" stammered Yong with a smile indicating his pleasure.

"In-ja, I inquired of the nurse about your brother, and she told me the family had moved. Have you returned permanently?"

Yong's rising voice showed his excitement at seeing his friend. When he saw the stares of other students, he became self-conscious, knowing that others were now aware of his interest in his visitor.

"Oh, Yong, you will not believe what happened. I told my father I wanted to attend this college. He said we would have to move, as he was being reassigned. Regardless, I made this school my first choice if my grades permitted. We moved, but I was very unhappy. My dear father saw my unhappiness and asked to be transferred back to his former job; we moved this week.

"Fortunately, they told me I could enroll here, but I will need much help since I'm far behind in my studies."

Yong needed to hear no more. "That's OK. I'll help you! I've had nothing to do but study since school began; it'll be good to have someone with whom I can study."

Thus began a grand experience for Yong. He had given up hope of seeing Yoo, In-ja again, and now they were fellow students. He knew it was a blessing of God!

With classes each day and hours in the library, it was difficult for Yong to find time for his Bible class, which now met on Saturday evenings. As the class was his link with his beginnings, Yong was faithful to make each session. That group of friends had been his best prayer partners, and his teacher had been a guiding light through many dark experiences.

Yong found physical and spiritual refreshment each week in worship. With his parents, Mr. Kim, Soon-sik, and, frequently, Hee-sung, a bench would be completely filled with those whom Yong loved dearly as they worshiped together.

Yong told his closest friend Soon-sik, "This is a wonderful way to start a busy week. God's spirit always gives me new strength and much reason to rejoice when I'm with family and friends in worship. I want you to pray with me that someday Yoo, In-ja will join us."

While at church, Yong remembered the spiritual needs of his Bible class friends and reflected on his spiritual journey. The one thing he wanted as much as a college education was to be a Christian who would bring honor to God.

In the beginning of his second year, Yong accepted the offer of Chang, Hee-sung to join the Christian club. Hee was now a senior.

The group studied the Bible, and on birthdays and other special occasions had small parties. They were a close group. Each day they prayed for an individual member of the club. Their regular meetings were held on Wednesdays. The club never led in popular campus activities; but they never failed to pray about such events.

From time to time, however, they would encourage some member to run for student body offices. Again, they never won, but they would get the attention of other students, frequently resulting in someone asking to join the club.

It had been rumored that Chang, Hee-sung was to represent the club and run for president of the student body. They had never had a candidate for president, as they always thought it would be easier to elect someone to the student council.

"Hee-sung, I've heard you're going to run for student body president. I want you to know I'll be praying for you to make a good impression for our Lord. We need to be able to have a good witness here on the campus. I asked Mr. Kim to pray for you; he said for me to encourage you to run for the office if you felt it was what God wanted you to do."

As Yong spoke, Yoo, In-ja joined the conversation. She was not a Christian; therefore, was not a member of the club. She and Yong had discussed Christianity a number of times. Her answer always related to the fact her father was Buddhist.

Her standard remark was, "I don't want to hurt his feelings by converting."

"Hee-sung, I want you to run for president. I'm not a Christian, but there are many like me and they'd vote for you." As In-ja spoke, it made a strong impression on Hee-sung. With his permission, the club recommended him for president the next day.

It came as a stunning surprise to see the influence and authority that Hee-sung wielded on campus. It was a difficult campaign with many campus demonstrations, some resulting in damages to people and property.

Hee had enlisted all of his Christian friends and made Yong something of an unofficial manager. When the votes had been counted, Hee told Yong, "You are one of the best campaign managers on campus."

Yong took charge of the volunteers and helped prepare posters and handbills. He seemed to know how to lead people, and as Hee had said, Yong became an outstanding political campaigner.

Hee won in a landslide. The campaign had been bitter for some. They could not understand how one of the least known groups on campus managed to influence so many people. They knew nothing of the prayer meetings or the early morning hours the Christians had met to organize, prepare advertisements, and meet with students to discuss the election.

Because of his work for Hee-sung, the name of Lee, Yong-soo became very prominent. One new approach Yong initiated was to send each student a personal postcard with a request to vote for Hee-sung. Each was signed by Yong.

This took much work and almost broke the club's treasury, but it made a deep impression on the students and faculty. Yong was asked to represent the Christian club on the student body planning and advisory group. This was a prestigious group that worked with the faculty and administration on events and plans for the students. The chairman was Dr. Song, the one who had remarked that Yong's recovery from the accident was a miracle. He was always kind to Yong and seemed to encourage others to listen to the counsel of the young Christian about student affairs.

Hee-sung graduated and was contemplating going to theological school. He stopped by Yong's house one evening to share the decision with the Lee family and discuss it in detail.

Yong knew Hee would make a good worker for the Lord, but had a word of advice for his friend. He asked gently if he could make his full feeling known.

Receiving an affirmative reply, Yong said, "Hee, it is not what you *want,* it is what God *directs.* If you feel God's spirit is calling you into His ministry, then you need to do as the Apostle Paul. Remember, he said he didn't confer with other humans about his call, just took God at His word there on the Damascus road and followed Him, even though he could not see, nor did he understand. That's what you've got to do too!"

"I appreciate your reminder, Yong," Hee-sung replied. "I felt that's what I should do. However, you've grown so much in the Lord, I just wanted to hear what you would say about my becoming a minister of the Lord."

Other discussion followed, with words of encouragement being given as Hee was leaving.

Looking directly at Yong, Hee said, "Brother in Christ, there's another matter we need to discuss. I have great hope for our school. There was much we couldn't get done last year. I've told friends and faculty members they should encourage you to run for president next year. We need to keep a Christian in important places of leadership if our school is to continue to be the best."

Those words humbled Yong; they were later repeated by Mr. Kim. He and Chang, Hee-sung had talked about Hee's decision. Hee-sung told Mr. Lee he was recommending Yong to run for president.

From time to time, Yoo, In-ja would echo Hee's remark. When

she mentioned it, Yong-soo would breathe a silent prayer for her salvation. He thought how good it would be if she became a full partner in the Christian enterprise. He was more interested in her conversion than in being student body president. When he told her this, she never seemed to understand it. Yong knew why, however, for as he had told Soon-sik on the fateful day down by the river, "When one becomes a believer in faith, understanding always follows."

As Yong began his senior year, he settled into a good routine. Frequently his professors asked him to lend his influence to some project in which they were interested. Much of his time was spent in counseling fellow students who wanted to see one thing or another take place on the campus.

As he made his way to his classes for the first time in the new school year, Yong felt much unrest on the campus.

He was now fully recovered from all traces of his accident, which seemed like a bad dream. The only bright thought about the entire experience was the memory of the wonderful Christians who befriended him.

The crowded days of classes, friends, club, library, counseling, and socializing left little time for other activities. Yet there was one thing that had caught Yong's attention.

A small group of students began handing out leaflets from the stairs of the main building. Each day they would have a new leaflet. The tenor of the messages was, Let's build a better nation. It was an attractive theme to Yong.

Each morning he found himself anxiously looking forward to the "Message of the Day," as the heading of the leaflet indicated.

The only author of the leaflet was Kim, and the name of the sponsoring group was new to him. It was the New Nation Coalition.

For three years Yong listened to the conversations of the students emphasizing need for improvement in the Korean government. There were those who were activists, not listening to any rational discussion of the current situation. They wanted confrontation and felt the student body should organize for direct action against those with whom they disagreed. They felt they could bring the government down by force and wanted everyone to help them.

This new group did not seem so radical. Yong had been careful not to be a part of those who were outspoken. He didn't want his club to get a reputation of being among the dissident. He felt Christians should be peacemakers.

Yong was never seen among those in campus demonstrations,

now a daily activity. This position was not popular, but it seemed prudent. The principle concern, Yong thought, was to be able to restore harmony and keep the school open and free.

Yoo, In-ja encouraged Yong to become a part of the movement. He resisted, telling her he had more important things to do.

Several times Yong inquired of his friends about the group calling itself the New Nation Coalition. None knew anything about it. As they were discussing it one day, a fellow student, whom Yong had never met, stepped forward. "I'm Paek, Ki-man. I understand that you're interested in our New Nation Coalition."

This took Yong by surprise. "Well, I've enjoyed what you've been writing in your leaflets. I'm interested in building a better nation. We've come a long way in the last 40 years in Korea, and we can always improve. We need to talk about it."

Paek, Ki-man introduced Yong to a couple of his friends, and one of them said he had used the name Kim in writing the leaflets, though that was not his name. Yong wondered why he needed an alias, but did not give it too much thought; he would remember this later.

The days for the elections were near. The Christian club invited Yong to represent them as Hee-sung had done previously. He could feel the influence of Hee and his words of encouragement when he received the invitation. Yet Yong had some real doubts.

Word spread as to who were candidate prospects. Many came to Yong expressing encouragement. Among that number were Paek, Ki-man and his two friends. Yong had never been able to determine the number in the new group that Paek represented.

Yong asked Ki-man for an appointment to discuss the details of the group's real purpose. Too, he wanted to know how many were in the new group.

At the appointed hour for the meeting, they gathered in the coffee shop in the basement of the bookstore building. Yong was surprised; the New Nation Coalition was still very small. In fact, it seemed the three he had previously met were the only members.

Paek, Ki-man spoke. "Lee, Yong-soo, you are a very important person on this campus. You don't know how influential you are, and it is good that you're not aware of your large following."

This shocked Yong. He wondered why such a bold statement had been made. He didn't have to wait long for the answer.

"Yong, we're in a position to make you a proposition that can be very profitable for you in the years ahead. Our cause is important. We have wealthy and influential people behind us; they have provided us with unlimited funds. We want one thing, and only one thing—we want a united Korea."

There was silence; Paek, Ki-man was measuring Yong's response. He looked intently into Yong's eyes. "You are the one who can help us get this student body and some influential professors behind our cause. This is the most prestigious school in Korea. If we can get this student body organized, there is no limit to what we can do."

As Ki-man finished, Yong was quick to ask, "Do? What do you want to do?"

"We want to see Korea unified. There are those who can do this with little or no effort, if the students demand it. We want you in your speech for student body president to put this idea forward. We need you to stand up and demand that our government sit down with other Koreans and make this a unified nation regardless of the cost. That's our idea of a new nation. You know there is a great ground swell for such a movement. Now is the time."

It was a fervent plea. Ki-man talked fervently for nearly an hour and answered most of Yong's questions with quick and conclusive answers.

In the final minutes of the conversation, all three offered their ideas to Yong about the prestige that would accrue to the one who made this possible on campus. The hint was given that Yong would never have to worry about finances, career, or future if the influential group of wealthy backers was pleased with his presentation.

A flood of rationalizing thoughts came to Yong as he rode to his home. He wanted Korea to be unified. There was not one word of strife or bloodshed. It sounded so peaceful and possible when it was discussed as to how it would come about.

Confiding later with Yoo, In-ja, he received further encouragement. She said she thought it was a way to get the money needed to launch a very successful career in business, or even graduate school. Such words made Yong's head spin, and he began to get a headache.

The speech was to be made in two days. Yong decided to miss his Wednesday Christian club meeting. He had a more important meeting on his mind, though he really needed to pray with his fellow Christians.

But he *had* to talk to Mr. Kim. Rushing out through the front gate of the campus, Yong told the taxi driver, "Imja Dong, and please hurry!"

In the small corner store, customers were coming and going as they did each day. Mr. Kim did not notice Yong; he was not expecting him. The two shared on Sundays when they met in church. Yong's studies and school activities kept him very busy. He seldom got to the store, even for short visits.

When Mr. Kim saw his young friend he shouted, "Why, Yong, what a happy surprise. What brings you home during this school day?" As Mr. Kim spoke, he noticed a deep furrow across Yong's forehead. It was not the young man he was accustomed to greeting.

"Well, sir, I just needed to talk to you, and it's important," Yong replied.

The customer he was serving left. Mr. Kim motioned for his young friend to take the chair at the table. "What is it, son? I know it's important if you've made a special trip."

Without preliminaries, Yong began. "Sir, a few weeks ago I became interested in some leaflets being given to students each morning by a new group on campus. The articles concerned unifying Korea. There was much in them about peace and unification through peaceful dialogue.

"Well," Yong continued without interruption from his friend, "last week I met one who claimed he was leader of the group and another who was doing the writing. Last night I had a meeting with them, and they made me a fantastic offer."

With that, Yong repeated all that Paek, Ki-man told him about the plans of the group. He gave the opinions of many of his friends, and especially that of his girlfriend, Yoo, In-ja, who had been most emphatic in her endorsement.

He concluded by saying that he was inclined to go along with them; not for personal gain, but because he really believed in what they seemingly wanted to achieve.

He added, "Mr. Kim, there is something about all of this which is confusing. I can't put my finger on it, but what I'm hearing and what I'm feeling are two different things. I really need help on this matter!"

Mr. Kim listened to the entire recitation. He dropped his head, as if in prayer for a moment, then began to speak slowly.

"Son, you know that you have been my very special friend for many years. God has had His hand on you from the first day of your salvation, even until now. He wants to be your Lord. There is little or nothing that you can do *for* God, the Creator of the universe. But, son, there's a great deal you can do *against* Him."

Yong's head now bowed. He listened with his heart. He heard his old friend continue. "Now, I want you to remember how you were saved. I want you to remember we studied about Pilgrim and how he became a Christian. Too, you will want to know today, and every day until eternity, that Mr. Kim did not make you a Christian. That was between you and God.

"I'm not going to tell you what *you* must do, but what I would do if I were in your place.

"I can't evaluate the offer. It may be valid and the best thing for the students and Korea. But you must decide, in prayer before God. You must remember, this is *your* pilgrimage, and God will hold you accountable for your decision. You must make it, no one else. I have confidence the Holy Spirit has your heart. If He didn't, you wouldn't be here today. So I'm going to trust God and you to make the right decision. I'll be praying for you!"

The conversation came to a close with a moment of prayer requested by Yong. He had gotten what he came for and expected. Giving a deep bow and words of appreciation, Yong indicated he would take a bus back to the campus. He needed time to do some praying and thinking.

The auditorium was crowded on the day of the campaign speeches. Not a seat remained vacant. Student candidate speeches were often held on the campus grounds, but on this day threatening weather dictated an indoor meeting.

Several made short speeches, stressing first one interest and then another. They represented many groups, and the office of president attracted all of them, even though they had little chance of winning.

The most powerful group on campus was the political science club. They had lost the presidency, being defeated by the small and seemingly insignificant Christian club the previous year. They intended to reverse the decision this year.

Their candidate gave a long and flowery speech. He made great promises and sought to become identified with all kinds of dissident groups. The students seemed to be moved. The political science club representative looked like he would recapture the high place this year.

Yong was the last candidate to speak. He was unaware the three members of the New Nation Coalition had alerted the student body with the statement, "Lee, Yong-soo is about to make the most important student speech every given on this campus." Experts at propaganda, the group was so effective it sensitized the entire student population as to the content of Yong's speech. The campus was alive with rumors and gossip.

When Yong stood, the students buzzed with anticipation; then grew strangely quiet. Yong addressed the school officials and officers of the student council. He then looked down to see Paek, Ki-man and his two friends on the front row of seats. They raised their hands to make a fist, rising from their seats shaking their heads in an affirmative manner, encouraging Yong to make a plea for their cause.

"Fellow students," Yong began slowly and deliberately, "I have been asked by the Christian club to represent them in a bid for the office of president of the student body. I am deeply humbled by this request and intended to come here today to discuss some serious matters with you that have been on my heart and mind for some time.

"My dear friend Chang, Hee-sung and I have discussed several matters that would make good topics for my appeal to you for your vote. However, I am going to ask you to permit me today to discuss a matter of far more serious consequence.

"A few days ago I was approached and asked to make this speech in favor of a certain group which has become popularly known for the leaflets it circulates each day. They felt my speech could consolidate you students into a group that would permit them to put their ideas into your minds and make this student body their tool. They gave me a very fascinating offer and a number of items they wanted included in my speech for the office of president of this fine student body."

Yong paused, looked straight into Ki-man's face, and continued. "When I was quite young, my grandmother died. I was deeply distressed by her death. A friend took me to a Christian church with him. I went, and two years later Jesus Christ became my Saviour. I became a Christian. For these years I have been studying and praying, desiring to become the kind of Christian that would bring glory to my Lord and Saviour."

The tears came to Yong's eyes. He paused, noticing no one now, but feeling the weight of his witness. He could not see the old gentleman who had made his way into the back of the auditorium, and who now leaned wearily against the wall.

If Yong had found the eyes of Yoo, In-ja who was seated on the back row, he would have noticed Mr. Kim, for he was standing directly behind her.

"Today I share with you my witness. Contrary to what some may think about me, my influence and witness are not for sale!

"We have a small nation here, but we are not small. God has blessed Korea beyond measure in these last 40 years. Now we must stand together to make our nation what God would have it become. To do this, we need a student body which will prayerfully support our elected leaders. They make mistakes; they are human; but they are free men and women, working to make our democracy pure and workable for all our people.

"We need to become the kind of men and women who will learn to kneel at the feet of our God, then go out and make this nation better. We need to sacrifice and pray to ensure a genuine freedom for our children. We need to pray for improvement, and hope that our Korean brothers to the north will put down their arms and join us in a peaceful venture to build a unified nation for the future.

"Christianity and godless communism are opposites. One cannot be a servant of Jesus Christ and a servant of communism. We must choose to stand opposed to all ideas that would make our nation anything but a glorious place where Jesus Christ may be served and the good news of His Resurrection is preached.

"The proposition I received from the group calling itself the New Nation Coalition was sophisticated and intriguing to young minds. It was veiled with a lucrative offer that would have made me wealthy.

"I was asked to become an enemy to all that God stands for in love and peace. *By God's grace, I will not compromise!*

"Your souls are precious; our freedom is precious; our way of life is precious. You are God's creation. Jesus Christ died for you, as He did for me. We must keep our land free that we may live to tell the world that Jesus' peace is the *only* peace.

"God bless you to stand tall by kneeling in your hearts before the Prince of Peace. Thank you very much!"

It was fiery. It was direct. It was a speech that caused the students to rise from their seats with a mighty ovation, though many had never been to a Christian church. They knew Yong was speaking of basic freedom: the freedom of religion, freedom of thought, and the right to personal pursuit of one's destiny.

As with a single mind, the students began a low chant, which was to lead to a cheer, repeating the name, "Yong-soo, Yong-soo!"

When the first chant began, a clear masculine voice raised with fervor was heard to come from the rear of the auditorium, "There's the youngest pilgrim!"

Yoo, In-ja heard it and spun around to look at the old gentleman who spoke the words; she did not recognize him. She had never met Mr. Kim.

As she rushed down the aisle to join her friend, tears which began during the speech now wet her face.

No one had expected Yong to make such an impassioned plea, but they were ready for it. The dissident voices and recent demonstrations had caused great unrest. The time for peace was at hand.

It was the time for Yong and those of his faith and generation to step into places of leadership.

"At first I thought you were a fool," In-ja almost shouted. Even though she spoke loudly, no one noticed. The students were still on their feet shouting and cheering. In-ja kept talking, a little louder now. "But, Yong, I'm proud of you, and you know I've been worried about what my father would think if I became a Christian. I should have been worried about what Christ was thinking and how I've been hurting Him. Yong, you've got to tell me again how to become a Christian!"

It was more than Yong could grasp. Hands were reaching out for him. He could not respond, for his prayers were being answered before his eyes. These were words he thought he would never hear from a beautiful young woman he hoped one day would be his wife.

There was much noise now; confusion reigned. Yong did not see the old man bent with the shape of years slowly making his way out of the auditorium. His face was wet too, but his heart was singing. It was strange, but the one tune that kept echoing through his head was: "Amazing grace! How sweet the sound, That saved a wretch like me! I once was lost, but now am found, Was blind, but now I see!"

As Mr. Kim eased down the long steps of the auditorium building, he was singing that song. Students paused to listen, but they could not hear the melody of song and prayer filling the heart of the singer.

Yong had but one thought. He remembered the night before when he had prayed almost all night about the speech. He remembered John Bunyan's Christian; how he had rolled his burden off at the cross, watching it roll down the hill into the open sepulchre, never to see it again. He thanked God in a quiet voice.

His moment of contemplation in the midst of voices and hands was interrupted. Paek, Ki-man was approaching. He was angry. Just as he began to speak, a hand took hold of his shoulder. The stranger who reached for Ki-man identified himself as an official of the national security agency.

Yong heard a few words that sounded like, "A warrant for your arrest for sedition and treason."

In that moment a flash of memory flooded Yong's mind. He

remembered a promise of God, as he thought how near he came to doing something that would have destroyed his witness and possibly the lives of others. He repeated it aloud, "I will never leave thee nor forsake thee."

These were the words which comforted the heart of the youngest pilgrim as he breathed a prayer of thanksgiving to his Lord, the One Whom he would serve forever.

Now there was one other matter to address. The assurance of acceptance of his friends and fellow students was great; yet nothing to compare with the victory of Jesus Christ in the life of Yoo, In-ja.

Taking her by the hand, Yong said, "In-ja, let's find a quiet place where we can study God's offer of salvation for you." It was that moment in the life of this young pilgrim when he knew two were about to become one forever in the sight of the Lord!